MW00425967

Dear Romance Reader,

Welcome to a world of breathtaking passion and never-ending romance.
Welcome to *Precious Gem Romances*.

It is our pleasure to present *Precious Gem Romances,* a wonderful new line of romance books by some of America's best-loved authors. Let these thrilling historical and contemporary romances sweep you away to far-off times and places in stories that will dazzle your senses and melt your heart.

Sparkling with joy, laughter, and love, each *Precious Gem Romance* glows with all the passion and excitement you expect from the very best in romance. Offered at a great affordable price, these books are an irresistible value—and an essential addition to your romance collection. Tender love stories you will want to read again and again, *Precious Gem Romances* are books you will treasure forever.

Look for fabulous new *Precious Gem Romances* each month—available only at Wal★Mart.

Kate Duffy
Editorial Director

AN OFFER OF OF MARRIAGE

Jo Ann Ferguson

Zebra Books
Kensington Publishing Corp.
http://www.zebrabooks.com

ZEBRA BOOKS are published by

Kensington Publishing Corp.
850 Third Avenue
New York, NY 10022

First Printing: September, 1999
10 9 8 7 6 5 4 3 2 1

Printed in the United States of America

For Neringa Bryant, Betsy Eliot, and Lori Lotti:
three of my favorite past presidents—and friends.

Prologue

The village smoldered in the setting sun. Death reeked in every breath the lad drew. Holding his sword at ready, he scanned the destruction. The dozen huts were funeral pyres of those who had called this place home.

He had seen death before . . . many times. He had come to recognize its varied faces. The gentle resignation when his grandmother had breathed her last. The furious refusal to surrender to death when the old *jarl* died of the wasting sickness that no warrior should suffer. The first time he had sliced into a deer and had watched blood slide in a warm river across his hands.

But this was different.

Running through the village set on the curve of a cove, he whispered a curse. Death in battle, death in a raid, that was the way of warriors. The village could have been overrun, its people cut down or stolen for slaves, and he would have understood. Death was a part of survival, for enemies could not be allowed to live. But this . . . Acrid bile filled his throat.

Another hut collapsed into the flames. He hurried to the scorched timbers, hoping, although he knew it was hopeless, that someone—anyone—remained alive.

"They forced them back into the burning buildings!" cried a shrill voice. "Instead of slaying them, they pushed them back into the fire."

He turned to look at the shaking woman who might be the only other survivor. He despised her cowardice, for she must have fled while the others had died in the blaze he had seen from where he was hunting in the forest. His fingers twitched by the hilt of his *hjör*. The long sword, which his father had given to him only a month ago on his eighth birthday, wished to savor the cold caress of revenge.

Embers rose and clung to his cross-gartered stockings and the hem of his short cloak as he rushed across the village. He had no time to listen to a coward's fear. Not now. Not when he needed to find . . .

He choked on the smoke which billowed around him like a dragon's fetid breath. When he saw a form on the singed grass, he inched forward. He did not want to look, but he must.

His stomach wrenched. This was what he had prayed he would not find. The woman's face was unrecognizable now, but he could recreate it in his mind. Laughing eyes, as blue as the river beneath a cloudless winter sky, and a smile that was warmer than a hearth fire. Her teasing laugh filled his ears, but only from memory. He would hear it no more.

A low moan battered his ears. A man, older than he by a generation, lay in the grass. He knelt next to a broken body.

"Father?" he whispered.

Tears glistened in his father's sea-green eyes, but none of them fell across his tanned face that had begun to wrinkle from exposure to sunlight and salt. "They raped her," he strained to say, each breath a battle.

"No, Father! It cannot be."

His father stared at the body of his wife. "Then they tossed her back into the fire because she refused to cower before them." He closed his eyes. "She will be welcomed among the bravest." He coughed, then groaned.

"Father, let me help you—"

"A warrior's death is mine, my son." His father clasped his hand. "A warrior's obligation is yours. You know what you must do."

"There is so much I need to learn. Father, stay with me. Fight with me!"

"The fight is yours."

The boy did not wipe away his tears. "Father, tell me what to do."

The man smiled through the blood washing across his face. "Have patience, son. Let your revenge be as merciless as this abomination against our family."

"Say what you wish me to do, Father."

"Do not rest until every last Englishman has paid for this. Go to the Norse king and give him your arm and your life." He quaked with pain. "Promise me this shall be so."

"I pledge it with my life, Father. I shall avenge what was done here today."

The old man smiled as he drew his last breath.

Standing, his son drew his dagger from his belt. He raised the *sax* to catch the sun. He did not flinch as he drew it across his left forearm. Scarlet flowed down his arm as he shouted his blood-oath to the sky. From this day, vengeance must be the only thing within his heart.

One

The spring wind blew sweet and warm, bringing the fragrance of salt from the sea and the portent of death. Once, the passing of winter had been a time for celebration as the days grew longer and the nights promised pleasure amid the soft grasses.

No longer.

Cyndra rubbed her fingers on the soaked blanket. One knuckle was bloodied, but all sensation had vanished in the icy water. Sitting on her heels, she sighed.

It should not be like this. They should greet spring's rebirth with delight. They should be able to wait to wash the winter's blankets until this brook warmed itself beneath the sun. Instead, spring brought darkness as the island waited in dread as the Norse scourge struck, destroying everything as it swept out of the sea like a storm-crazed wave.

"May they all be cursed," she whispered as she lifted the blanket. Her muscles strained, for the thick wool fought her as fiercely as her father battled the Norse.

"Milady?"

At the shout, she looked over her shoulder, keeping one hand on the stubborn blanket. A dark-haired lad raced along the bank, drawing the attention of the women who worked beside her.

"What is it, Nyle?" A cramp knotted her lower back.

Fear glowed in the lad's eyes. "Riders! A dozen or more!"

"How far away are they?" Cyndra tore her gaze from his frightened face to scan the horizon where the sea merged with the sky. It was empty. No Viking ships waited to spew their pestilence upon the shore. Praise all the saints!

"Close behind me."

She heard a woman's moan and fought the temptation to surrender to fear. "Hide! Do not let them see you!"

Their faces bleached with fear, the women scurried away. The earliest lesson taught within Manor Saeburgh was to obey that order. Vikings thought only of riches and women and battle. Those who hid might escape their savagery.

"Hurry, milady!" whispered her maid Gleineth, her eyes nearly popping from her face.

"Go!"

Gleineth raced behind a thicket.

Putting a stone on the sodden blanket to keep it from floating away, Cyndra started to rise. She froze as she heard hoofbeats. Through a break in the trees, riders sped toward her in a cloud of dust. Sunlight glinted on the swords they wore at their sides, and their faces were hidden by leather helmets.

She looked both ways along the shore. Where could she hide? *Do not be afraid to be bold in battle.* Her father's voice, repeating the lesson he had been teaching her younger brother, rang through her head.

She did not hesitate. Flinging herself down behind a massive boulder closer to the road, she clung to the earth like a dying man holding onto life. She hoped her dark gown and veil would make her vanish within the afternoon shadows. She pressed her face against her hands and tried to remember how to pray.

She heard nothing but the hoofbeats. Holding her breath, she waited for them to pass. *Go by without seeing us. Please do not see us.* Even if these men were not enemies, strangers were not welcome.

Her breath burned in her chest as the riders slowed. Curse her eyes, she had thought about saving the blankets when she should have let them swirl away. Now the blankets might betray them. Her fingers curled into fists.

Go on. Do not see us.

A man shouted something, and another answered as the hoofbeats drew even with her. She could not understand their words over the thud of her heart. Father's face and Sigestan's burst into her mind. Thank the saints, her brother had not come with them today.

Terror strangled her as something tapped her on the shoulder. She looked up, the sun blinding her. A broadsword! She peeked over the boulder to see a rider in a brown cloak peering at her from his horse. His face was lost beneath his cowl. Behind him, his comrades edged their horses forward to stare at her from behind the menacing anonymity of their helmets. He motioned with the sword for her to rise.

Not faltering, Cyndra stood. She must keep these

men from finding the others. She put her hand on the knife in her girdle. She heard a low chuckle and stiffened. Her blade was scant defense against so many warriors, but her feeble resistance might give the other women a chance to flee.

The lead rider pushed back his cowl and drew off his helmet to reveal the rugged lines of his bronzed face. Sunlight shone through the black hair that brushed his collar. He had not thrown his cloak aside, but Cyndra could see that his body was straight and strong. This man was warrior bred and trained, bringing death to his enemies and comfort to his allies. She wished she knew which he would consider her.

Her eyes were caught by his. They were the hue of a calm sea, but nothing was tranquil about the emotions in them. This man was as threatening as the broadsword he slid into a loop on his saddle. His lips tilted in a cool smile as his gaze glided along her with the intimacy of a forbidden caress. Her skin burned in its wake as every instinct beseeched her to turn and run.

She could not run. She must give the others a chance to escape, even if she could not.

The slow smile warmed his hard face as he leaned his helmet on his saddle and folded his arms atop it. Her heart halted in midbeat, for his fingers still rested on the hilt of his sword. "We are well met on this splendid day on Ealdorman Edgar's lands," he said in English, not some barbaric Norse tongue; but the Vikings were not her father's only enemies.

"Greetings to you, traveler." Cyndra must guard what she said until he identified himself.

"Seeing you here tells me we are not far from a village or manor."

She would not be tempted by his smile into betraying the truth. "Many live in the forest, traveler."

"Outlaws and landless fools who have lost their honor." In a motion too quick for her to counter, he rode forward and grasped her hand. He tugged her toward the horse. "I would label you neither, for you have the stance of a law-abiding woman."

She wanted to retort, but trembled as he held her to his thigh, which was as hard as the rocks. Scents of horseflesh and dust drifted from him. She gasped when his arm drew her even closer so her breasts pressed against his leg. The fear that flashed through her was not cold, but as hot as the heart of a fire.

His laugh resonated with the power of the watch's call to battle. "And I suspect, by your reaction, you still possess a maiden's honor."

Raising her gaze up to his, she knew she was right to be wary. Amusement glistened in his eyes; but stronger, more savage emotions burned there as well. He had held the sword with the ruthlessness of a man who would grant his enemies no clemency.

"What do you want?" she whispered.

He grinned. "You should take care, pretty one, when you pose such a beguiling question."

Cyndra snatched her hand away as she heard another rumble of laughter from his men. By the saints, she had forgotten how many were witnessing this. Not only the men, but her women. If word of this reached her father's ears, he might begin to think anew of finding her a husband before her own foolishness led her into trouble.

Lifting her chin, she folded her arms. "You spoke of Ealdorman Edgar. Are you his allies?"

"Would you demand proof of that allegiance if I tell you *yes?*"

"I would ask why you ride through his lands."

"That, pretty one," he replied, resting his arms on his helmet once more, "is a matter not meant for your ears." Glancing past her, he added, "Or for the ears that are concealed by brush and rock and are struggling to catch every word we speak. Your allies, I suspect, for you have been careful not to look in their direction."

Had he seen the women, or was this a ploy to persuade her to expose them? "As you have said nothing worth retelling, you need have no worry."

His laugh was unrestrained. "Well said, pretty one. I would that I had time to share with you words and more." Again his gaze swept over her as if it could peel away the layers of her gown. Regret sifted into his voice. "It cannot be, for our thane gave us orders to ride without delay to Manor Saeburgh to deliver his message to his ally Ealdorman Edgar." He smiled. " 'Twould be easier to obey such a command if we knew the location of that manor."

"You speak of alliance without disclosing your thane's name."

"True." He leaned forward and brushed a strand of her hair back from her face.

She batted his hand away. A mistake, she feared, when his eyes narrowed in an icy stare. She opened her mouth to warn him that the ealdorman's daughter was not accustomed to such coarse treatment. She must not let him goad her into revealing more than she should.

Wiping her hands on her work-stained gown, she said, "Both the ealdorman's friends and foes know the way to Manor Saeburgh is to follow this road toward the sea. Once you have passed this copse, you will see the tower of Manor Saeburgh rising above the palisades. It is a sight to chill the ambitions of his enemies."

"A warning?"

"The truth."

"I shall take it as the warning you intended, pretty one. We shall ride on without pausing to water our horses, for I suspected the manor was not far as soon as I saw such a fair gathering here."

Cyndra frowned as she heard a twitter of laughter behind her. She glanced back to discover the others had emerged. They should know better than to trust a stranger simply because he had a smile that twisted a woman's mind in the very direction of his own.

" 'Tis a shame we have no time to play hide-and-seek with you and your companions," the man said. Lifting her hand, he brushed it with his lips. "Or any other games."

She snatched her hand away before she could reveal how his brazen kiss sent heated shivers careening through her. "We have no time for such absurd fancies."

"A pity, pretty one, for both of us. Mayhap some other time when both of us are done with distasteful chores."

"Distasteful?" Cyndra's stomach cramped with sudden fear. "Do you bring bad news to Manor Saeburgh?"

"As I said, that is not for your ears. I bid you good day, pretty one. May we meet again when our obligations are behind us." He set his helmet on his head. Raising his hand, he shouted a command. The horses and their riders sped out of sight around a bend in the road.

Cyndra stared after them. *Distasteful?* What task did the king have now for her father? What more could Ethelred ask of her father, who had faithfully protected this part of the king's realm?

"Milady?"

She did not turn to Gleineth. She closed her eyes and uttered a prayer that King Ethelred had not surrendered England to the Norse.

"Did you see how strong they are?" Gleineth asked. "Not a shoulder bent among the lot, and they must have ridden far."

"Do you think so?"

The redhead grinned. "Did you not notice the dust upon him, milady?" She pointed to Cyndra's gown. "And upon you, milady."

Cyndra hastily brushed the telltale dirt from her damp gown. That man, who had not given her the courtesy of his name, had tried to beguile her and, she had to admit, almost succeeded. Good looks were not the only thing she wanted in the man she would let woo and wed her. He must be as brave and loyal and as utterly honest as her father. No keen-witted stranger would change her mind about that.

She flinched when she heard her servants lauding the strangers and wondering aloud if they would remain at Manor Saeburgh for more than one night. Reprimanding the women was useless. No doubt, Gleineth had been the first to come out from her hiding place. Her maid enjoyed flirting with the guards along the wall.

Cyndra walked back to the brook and lifted the rock off the blanket. Yanking the drenched wool out of the water, she glanced over her shoulder to see Gleineth giggling. Cyndra should find Gleineth a husband, but any wedding would remind Father that his only daughter remained unmarried.

Why was it the lot of daughters to marry and move far from their beloved homes? Touching the linen girdle at her waist, her fingertips brushed the ring of iron keys attached to it. She had a home, which her father and younger brother needed her to oversee, and she had no interest in a husband.

She frowned as she heard the women continuing to discuss the strangers. Unexpected guests traveling at such a speed often heralded evil tidings. Again she looked through the trees to the sea.

Curse the Vikings! They were not satisfied with carving out their own kingdom on England's eastern shore, enslaving the English who lived there. Now they sought to conquer the rest of England. Never! Never, never would the daughter of Ealdorman Edgar bend her knee to a Viking overlord.

And, she thought, her smile returning, she would never bend her knee to an unwanted husband. Father had promised her that when the first man came to ask for her hand before her twelfth birthday. She must marry or take her vows in the convent on the hill inland from Manor Saeburgh, but she could choose her own husband. Father would hold that pledge as dear as he did his oath to see the Norse washed back into the sea that spawned their wickedness.

Two

Brenwyn threw his cloak back over his right shoulder to keep his sword arm free as he drew in his horse at the gate of Manor Saeburgh. He kept his hand on the hilt of his sword while he admired the palisades and the defenses along it. It was no wonder that the king depended on his loyal ealdorman to do what Ethelred could not.

Ethelred was a useless king in a time when England needed a leader as strong as the legendary Arthur. Again Brenwyn appraised the wall. If Ethelred did not lose his kingdom before this year came to a close, it would be because of Ealdorman Edgar and the few other men of courage like him.

And women of courage. He let a smile tip his lips as he let his thoughts linger on the comely lass who had faced him bravely by the stream. If all the women within Ealdorman Edgar's land were so valiant and beautiful . . . Just touching a lock of her golden hair had bedeviled him into wanting to caress her far less chastely. Her ardent answers suggested a sweeter passion that he might find upon her lips.

"Who goes?" came the call from the sentry on the wall.

He thrust aside thoughts of the tempting lass. "Brenwyn of Manor Darburgh, who leads Thane Morcar's men."

"Darburgh?" The sentry peeked over the crenelated top with a ragged-tooth sneer. "Again?"

With effort, Brenwyn kept his smile in place. Morcar must have known how humiliating this visit would be, so the thane had sent Brenwyn to present his request. As a ceorl, Brenwyn could not defy his thane's orders.

Not openly.

"Yes, again," he answered.

"Enter!" called the sentry, his laughter bringing a grumble from the men behind Brenwyn.

Without turning, he snapped an order to Cerdic, his second-in-command. Nothing must interfere with delivering this message, even though, if all went as Brenwyn anticipated, upon their return to Manor Darburgh, Morcar would be looking for someone to blame for this failure. The thane would make certain whoever was the focus of his rage suffered such torment that death would seem a welcome release.

The men were silent as they entered the courtyard. They swung down from their horses when he did. Brenwyn grasped his sword and slid it into the belt that hung from the strap looped across his chest. He did not look back as he strode past the thatched roofs of byres and kitchens toward the bridge over the inner moat and up the steep mound to the great hall's brightly painted tower. His men would do as he had trained them. They, too, knew the cost of failing today.

Cerdic whistled quietly. When Brenwyn glanced at the man whose brown hair brushed his shoulders that were as broad as a bull's, Cerdic said, "Morcar could learn much from this burgh."

Brenwyn nodded as he scanned the courtyard and the mound that was far higher than the one within Manor Darburgh. From the top of the tower, a look-out could keep watch on more than a league of the shore and the pair of streams that were deep enough for a *drakkar,* a Viking long ship.

Brenwyn smiled as he saw three well houses. Ealdorman Edgar had prepared his manor for battle or siege. No wonder, Morcar wanted the ealdorman's favor. Any victory here would bring glory to everyone connected with Edgar.

"Let's be done with this disgusting task," he said as he motioned for Cerdic to follow.

"You know what the ealdorman will say."

Brenwyn clapped his friend on the back. "Let me enjoy the chance to hear it, so I might savor every word before I share them with Morcar."

"Do not be a fool! Morcar will not take kindly to what he must hear."

"I know." He motioned toward the mound. "Therefore, we might as well enjoy what little pleasure there is in this."

Cerdic's only answer was a discouraged sigh.

Brenwyn cursed. He had worked with Morcar's *fyrd* to build up their confidence in their arms and their wits. Morcar, with his tempers which often ended with yet another good man dead, could destroy that with a single word. It was Brenwyn's misfortune that he had to stay and suffer along with those who served with him.

Aware of eyes aimed at his back, he did not slow as he climbed the almost vertical steps. He must think of his duty instead of the lovely lass by the stream. Her sparkling eyes, her slender hands which suggested that the form beneath her bulky gown was as shapely, and her quick wit had urged him to lure her to a shadowed forest bower.

Cerdic whistled again as they entered the great hall. Its roof climbed far higher than Manor Darburgh's. Small windows with thick shutters broke the timbered walls, and brands were nailed to the upper boards to be lit when no sunlight came through the arched doorway. Along the longer walls, beneath shields and battle-axes, benches waited for the ealdorman's men. Furs and wool blankets were stacked on one. In the center of the floor, a circular hearth was unlit. He glanced at the hole in the roof. Smoke would swirl up through it to flavor the air in the sleeping rooms above before escaping through the thatched roof.

He wondered which bench served as a bed for the pretty wench. Her cheeks had been a winsome pink beneath the few vagrant strands of hair which were as golden as the specks in her intriguing brown eyes. Had he been correct when he called her a maiden, or did a man share her bench? The ealdorman's hospitality would allow Morcar's men to remain here for a night. That sweet lass could help him forget muscles that ached from his long journey as her lithe fingers stroked him.

" 'Tis even grander than rumor suggested," Cerdic murmured, tearing Brenwyn from his fantasy.

Before he could reply, footsteps sounded. A page stepped into the great hall to intone, "Ealdorman Edgar." He moved aside to let a man enter.

The ealdorman was not tall. The gold brooch he wore at his shoulder denoted his wealth and his rank. Gray twisted through his hair and tinted his full beard. All the lines in his face did not come from age, for Brenwyn recognized the jagged scars left by a honed blade. Ealdorman Edgar had fought hard to hold here; and he would, Brenwyn knew, die before relinquishing this land.

In the ealdorman's wake walked a pale-haired lad who could be no more than thirteen. Brenwyn guessed the boy was Sigestan, Edgar's heir. He was built as solidly as his father, but already stood a half head taller. His hand rested on his sword, warning he was prepared to defend his father and the manor.

"I bring you greetings from Thane Morcar," Brenwyn said as he knelt.

"Morcar?" the ealdorman demanded. "What does that witless coward wish of me now?"

Brenwyn drew a rolled page from beneath his cloak. Rising when Edgar motioned, he fought to hide his smile as the ealdorman threw the parchment onto the floor and strode to the raised table at the end of the great hall.

"This is an outrage!" Edgar snarled. "Another petition to marry my daughter Cyndra? For a third time, he makes this request? What sort of fool does he consider me?"

Brenwyn did not reply as Ealdorman Edgar paced behind the raised table. If Morcar had the wit of a frog, he would have known this would be the ealdorman's answer. The ealdorman should be furious at such a ridiculous petition from an honorless man like Morcar of Manor Darburgh. Brenwyn would gladly have told his thane that, but Morcar would never seek—or heed—the counsel of a ceorl.

"What excuse does Morcar give for sending such a request when I have denied his petition twice already?" asked Edgar.

"He has heard much of your daughter's beauty, and he wishes to express his great desire to make her his adored wife." The hypocritical words were as bitter as nettles on his tongue. "Morcar believes a match between him and your daughter will forge a great alliance for England."

"Does he believe that?"

"Yes."

Edgar paused and leaned his fists on the table. "Do you?"

Brenwyn folded his hands behind his back, astonished that the ealdorman had asked him. "You want my opinion, milord?"

"You know Morcar well, for you serve him. Do you think such a marriage would help England?"

"It would help Morcar." He smiled as the ealdorman laughed.

"Well said." Edgar eyed him up and down. "Speak your name."

"Brenwyn, ceorl in service to Thane Morcar." He gestured toward Cerdic. "This is—"

"He sends a *ceorl* to negotiate for my daughter's hand?"

Brenwyn was accustomed to the insult. A ceorl held the lowest of free ranks; but, for now, this life suited him.

"I lead Morcar's *fyrd.*"

"A ceorl leads his warriors?" Sigestan blurted. His voice was still as high as a child's.

"Morcar has no brave son to serve him as the leader of his *fyrd.*"

"And so he wants to marry my sister to get an heir to do what he fears to do himself?" The lad slammed his fist into the table. "Father, you cannot heed this petition."

"You worry needlessly, son." Edgar's smile was as cold as a Norse winter. "The answer to Morcar's petition is *no*. Take my answer to Morcar, and tell him not to bother me again. My daughter will never—"

"Will never what, Father?" interrupted a light voice that flowed through Brenwyn like molten silver.

When Cerdic mumbled a fervent prayer, Brenwyn stared at the lass he had spoken to by the stream. *She* was the ealdorman's daughter? Had he been so blinded by her warm eyes and delicate features that he had not noted the keys at her slender waist that bespoke her place as the manor's lady? Mayhap he had, for her eyes scintillated like the sun on the crest of a wave as she held up her hand to her father. Recalling those fingers in his, he swallowed the craving that could never be sated. A serving wench might have been his for the night, but a ceorl could not aspire to possess an ealdorman's daughter.

The ealdorman smiled when he took his daughter's hand and drew her up to stand beside him. Brenwyn understood the pride in Edgar's eyes and the avarice in Morcar's. Bravely she had faced him and his warriors alone. She was beautiful, with a sensuality in every motion that enticed a man to think of other motions he would like to share with her. When she kissed her father on the cheek, Brenwyn wondered how those lips would taste against his.

This exquisite woman could not be his, and she must not be Morcar's. He wondered what promises of gold that old toad had offered Ealdorman Edgar. Let Morcar look elsewhere for the mother of the heir that his previous wives had failed to give him. Lady Cyndra was too strong to submit to Morcar's will and too fragile to fight the thane's brutality.

"My daughter, I fear you interrupt us at our business," the ealdorman said with another chuckle. His smile included the lanky serving-woman who stood beside Lady Cyndra. "Gleineth, I had hoped you could inspire your lady to have patience."

"Do not scold Gleineth, for I was eager to see what tidings the travelers bring." Cyndra smiled as she sat. Relief coursed through her at her father's laugh and her brother's smile. Father would not be in a jovial mood if this stranger brought bad news.

When the stranger's gaze met hers, she gripped the table, glad its breadth was between them. His smile was warm, but she could not silence the small voice that whispered, *Stay away from this man.*

Sigestan said, "Ceorl Brenwyn and his companions bring only old news, Cyndra."

"Ceorl?" She shut her mouth when she saw emotions flare in the dark-haired man's eyes. Anger or something else? She could not tell. This man was a ceorl? A man with his strength and the obvious respect he garnered from his men should have gained the lands and prestige to win the title of thane.

Brenwyn said, bowing his head to her, "We are well met again, milady."

"Again?" asked Father.

Cyndra smiled at him, glad for the excuse to avoid Brenwyn's compelling gaze. "While we were washing blankets, Brenwyn asked for directions here."

"And received, from your gracious daughter, excellent ones, as you can see, milord," Brenwyn added.

Father put his hand on her shoulder. "She was gracious because she did not realize you ride on the orders of Thane Morcar."

"Morcar?" Her nose wrinkled. "Again? Will he not learn that I have no interest in marrying him?"

Laughter startled her. She looked at the two men from Manor Darburgh and wished she had not when her gaze was caught anew by Brenwyn's. He was a ceorl, she reminded herself. She should not be thinking of how his hand had held hers in a tender prison and of how his strong leg had sent luscious warmth through her.

"I applaud your good taste, milady," Brenwyn said.

Her father's chuckle freed Cyndra to look away. "Again well said. Ceorl Brenwyn, you and your companions are welcome to remain here tonight, unless you must return without delay."

"We are grateful for your benevolence, milord." Brenwyn bowed his head and motioned for Cerdic to take that message to the other men. "We have no need to hurry back to Manor Darburgh, for Morcar is away on the king's business."

The ealdorman sniffed his disgust. "Mayhap the two of them can devise a single worthwhile idea between them. Come, Sigestan. Important matters await our attention."

Sigestan winked at Cyndra. As the sound of his steps disappeared, she sighed into the silence. Father had the skills of a diplomat as well as a warrior, but he could not repress his opinions of King Ethelred.

"Father is still rankled," she said quietly, "by the king's failure to listen to his Witan."

"It does seem ridiculous for Ethelred to call together a council of wise men and ignore their advice," Brenwyn replied, loosening his cloak and letting it fall over his arm.

His mail showed signs of recent repair. A ceorl could not afford better than another's castoffs. But the sword he wore at his side glittered, even in the dim light. It had been made by a gifted swordsmith.

"We can only pray for the king to gain the wisdom he needs to keep England safe," Gleineth said softly, warning Cyndra she had waited too long to answer.

Brenwyn chuckled. "Or for another king."

Cyndra stared, astonished. "You speak treason, Brenwyn."

He smiled. "I speak only what is in the minds of many who are afraid to voice the truth."

"By all the saints, you dare much."

"It is easy to dare much when there is so little left to lose."

Cyndra wished she had left with Father and Sigestan, for she did not want to admit her thoughts had often strayed in such disloyal directions as well. Better to ask simple questions that could lead to simple answers. "Will you be staying the night?"

When he leaned one elbow on the table and smiled, his gaze moved along her in a slow caress. "Your kind invitation is one I would be a fool to refuse," he murmured as his hand splayed across the table to a finger's breadth from hers.

The warmth leaped from his skin to hers like lightning arcing across a summer sky. She pushed herself to her feet. "It was my father's invitation to spend the night within our walls."

"That is true. It is also true that the lord may offer, but 'tis the lady of the manor who must satisfy the needs of those guests." With a chuckle, he stepped back.

She started to answer, then scowled. What was amiss with her? She was letting Gleineth's babbling about flirtations taint her mind. As the lady of the manor, she should set the limits on how far such harmless banter should go. But how could she when everything she said was turned by Brenwyn into an invitation to delight?

"You are bold," she said.

"I am honest, milady. I try always to be as honest as I can and still serve my sword-sworn oath."

Coming down from behind the table, she said, "Then I shall be as honest. My father would have your tongue if he heard you speak as you have, even in jest."

"I shall be certain he is not a witness to my honesty, even in jest." He bowed and walked toward the door, leaving her to wonder if his words were a barely veiled threat or a promise of pleasure yet unknown.

Three

The gnarled hand reached out through the half-closed gate and took the basket Cyndra held. It drew back within the shadows as a hushed voice whispered, "The abbess told me to thank you, milady, and to tell you that we shall include a special prayer for your family at vespers tonight."

Cyndra smiled as she took an empty basket. The gatekeeper at the convent murmured the same words each week when Cyndra brought fresh eggs here. Stepping aside to let Sigestan hand over his baskets of meat and bread, she heard the sister's blessing on them for their generosity. Never had that blessing seemed so comforting.

One of her earliest memories was coming here with her mother before the fever had taken Lady Elva. Every week, in memory of her mother, she made the journey up the hill behind Manor Saeburgh and down into the narrow valley. Usually she made the pilgrimage alone, but sometimes, Sigestan came with her. When he did, she knew he wished to speak to her without anyone else hearing.

He remained silent as they turned their backs on the weathered gate and the rising sun. He rocked a pair of baskets, warning that, today, what he wanted to say was important.

As they climbed the hill, Cyndra asked, "What is amiss, Sigestan?"

"That Morcar continues pestering Father with petitions."

She laughed, for she had expected something far more consequential. "Morcar of Manor Darburgh has a reputation which does not entice a maiden's heart."

"He is a cowardly dog."

"We are in agreement, so do not let this trouble you."

"You sound like Father." He paused as they reached the trees at the crest. Snow still clumped where the sun did not reach. "But, Cyndra, when I think of your leaving us . . ."

"I am not leaving now or anytime soon."

"But the time will come when you must leave."

"I know." Cyndra walked through the chilly shadows. "Just remember that Father has granted me the privilege of selecting the man I wish to wed."

"A man like Brenwyn of Manor Darburgh?"

Shock pierced her as she whirled to look back at Sigestan. She almost accused him of seeing into last night's dreams, when the ceorl's enigmatic smile had led her into a perilous enchantment as his fingers sought to arouse sensations she had not guessed existed. Sensations that had left her covered with a sheen of perspiration when she woke, her blanket tangled about her as his body had been in the dream.

"Cyndra?"

She smiled weakly. "Forgive me. My thoughts were elsewhere."

"Upon Brenwyn?"

"What makes you say that?"

"I have seen the expression a man wears when he wants a woman." He dug his toe into the half-frozen dirt. "Brenwyn wore that expression when he looked at you last night."

"It means nothing." She could not speak of how something had fluttered inside her each time Brenwyn had glanced in her direction while the household talked with the travelers who brought news from beyond Manor Saeburgh. And Brenwyn had glanced at her often.

Cyndra clasped the basket more tightly as she hurried to where the trees would thin along the path leading to the manor's walls. Brenwyn would be leaving today, and they would never see him again.

Sigestan hurried to catch up with her. "Forgive me."

"Why does Brenwyn concern you so?"

"Because he is lying." He curled his fingers around the basket handles. "If a ceorl within our walls spoke with such intelligence, Father would raise him in rank."

"You must not judge other manors by what we know here."

"You are again echoing Father."

"Because it is true." She motioned along the road. "We cannot linger here. Too much waits to be done."

"More blankets to clean?"

"You may laugh, Sigestan, but, if you had to . . ." Cyndra stared at the evergreens ahead of them. Had one moved even though no breeze came off the sea?

"What is it?"

"I thought—" She shook her head. If something

lurked within the shrubs, the beast was hiding, afraid of them. " 'Tis nothing."

"If you do not want to do the blankets," he said, rocking the baskets to match his steps, "you need only give directions to the ceorls' women to do them."

"The manor's lady asks nothing of others that she is not willing to do herself."

"You are quoting Father again." He laughed. "No wonder he scolds me, telling me that I must heed more closely the wisdom he has to pass onto me. You learned it all with ease."

She linked her arm through his, amazed as she had been for the past year that she had to look up to meet his eyes. "You learn different lessons, Sigestan. Lessons of war and diplomacy and the value of what we grow and sell."

"All of which you know." He cocked his head and grinned. "Many times I have wished *you* were the son."

"You will make a splendid ealdorman when your time comes. If—"

A branch cracked.

"What was that?" His voice broke as he pulled his sword. "Have mercy on our souls!"

Cyndra whirled. She gripped his arm as she stared at the man leaping from the bushes. By all the saints! A Viking!

"Warn Father!" With a shriek, Sigestan ran to meet the sword wielded by the man who was more than twice his width.

She stared when the man screamed in agony, then fell to the earth. She tried to move. She was as frozen as the stream in winter. He was dead! Sigestan had killed him.

"Cyndra! Run! Get help!"

Her brother's voice shattered her terror. She turned and screamed as she saw two more Vikings. They were encircled by enemies.

She spun to flee into the woods. A vicious shove sent her reeling into a boulder. She stared along a deadly axe and up a brawny arm to meet the satisfied smile of a wide-shouldered man. Beneath his metal helmet, on either side of the carved nosepiece, his eyes burned with blood-lust. Scarlet glistened on his mail.

English blood!

"No," she moaned as she looked toward the manor. Flames exploded through the lower bailey, and screams rose to torture her ears. In the river, she saw three Viking ships.

She heard her brother shout.

"Sigestan!" She moved, but the axe pricked her gown.

The Viking snarled something.

She shook her head. Even if she understood his pig squealings, she would never agree. She locked eyes with him. If he thought she would plead for her life, he was wrong. The daughter of Ealdorman Edgar would never beg for mercy from a Norse monster. She turned so he could not see the knife in her girdle or how her hand settled on its haft.

Grabbing her shoulder, he pushed her against the rock. She called out her father's name and raised the knife. It sliced into his upper arm. She pushed past him. He caught her in a steel grip. Muttering something in his heathen tongue, he thrust her back. She hit the rock again. Hard. Agony exploded in her head.

She dropped to her knees, struggling to hold onto

her senses. Dear God, nothing had ever hurt like this. She screamed when the Viking jerked her to her feet and lifted the bloody knife.

Slowly he lowered it, only inches from her face. He held the flat of the blade against her cheek. She stared straight ahead, holding what might be her final breath.

With a roar, he raised the knife and slashed down. She screamed. When her linen girdle fell, sliced through, he seized it and ripped the iron ring off. He shouted with triumph.

She stared at him. Was that all he wanted? Her keys? She tried to edge away.

He grasped her and pulled her veil off her hair. Now the lust in his eyes was not for blood.

"No!" she cried. "Let me go!"

He tugged her to him, the sharp rings of his mail cutting into her. She struck him with her fists. Laughing, he gripped her face. Terror that dimmed everything she had known before halted her heart in midbeat as he forced her mouth under his. Her stomach threatened to erupt when he pressed her back against the boulder.

"Release her! Now!"

The Norseman twirled her in front of him.

"Sigestan!" she cried. "For the love of heaven, save yourself!"

The arm tightened around her. She groaned when the Norse dog growled and shook her as if she were a downed bird.

Sigestan hoisted his sword, but it fell as astonishment wiped the rage from his face. His eyes rolled as he pitched forward. Behind him, another Norseman stood, his sword dripping blood. Her brother's blood!

"No!" Cyndra shrieked. "Sigestan! Sigestan!"

Her captor laughed as he spun her back to him, then screeched when she raked her nails down his face. He pushed her to the bloody ground. He grasped the front of her torn gown, and she moaned in horror.

Suddenly he released her. Steel clashed over her head in a single blow. A man shouted a command she could not understand through her ringing ears. Her eyes refused to focus. But a single thought remained.

Sigestan!

She clawed at the earth, trying to reach him. Another moan burst from her when she was turned onto her back. Arms swept beneath her, lifting her against a chest as hard as the boulder. Mail pricked her cheek.

"No!" she screamed. She raised her fists.

"Milady, do not fight your ally."

She blinked. Above taut lips, Brenwyn's sea-blue eyes were slitted in anger. But not at her, she realized, as he stared around them.

"How . . . why are you here?" She shuddered. "You should be fighting within the manor."

"When I heard you were outside the walls, I knew what you could be facing."

"There were so many Vikings. You could have been killed."

"I wanted to be sure you were not."

She sagged against his chest. "We must hide."

"Fear not; they are fleeing."

"Fleeing?" She tried to peer past him. "Why would they leave now?"

He laughed stiffly. "You have little faith in the

men who have pledged their arms to your father, milady."

"Father? Is Father alive?"

"I am not certain who lives."

She closed her eyes, seeking what strength she had left. "You risked your life to come here."

He set her on her feet and tilted her face toward him. "No man, be he Norse or English, should hurt you."

She winced when he touched her aching cheek. "Do not apologize. I am alive. Bruising my face would have been the least of his crimes if you had not halted him."

"I know, milady." Fury blazed in his eyes. "But they are gone, and you are alive."

"I thank you, Brenwyn," she said, putting her fingers on his arm. When he winced, she pulled back. "Are you hurt?"

"Not badly. It can wait. We should see to others who are hurt worse."

"Sigestan!" She ran to where her brother had not moved. She knelt and ran her hand along his back, seeking the beat of his heart. "He lives. We must get him help."

When Brenwyn did not answer, she realized he was staring at the sea. She followed his gaze, and her breath stuck in her throat.

The outer walls of the burgh were burning ruins. A keening cry rose on the wind. Even from here, she could see corpses littering the courtyard. The lower bailey was aflame. The bridge to the inner mound lay on its side, the supports snapped. Only the tower at the top still stood, although arrows stuck to it, making it look like a hedgehog.

And where the river emptied into the sea, the Viking ships sailed away.

They would return. She was as certain of that as she had been certain her father would defeat them. As she *had been* certain. Now she was sure of nothing save that the Norse scourge would return and . . . She hid her face in her hands and wept.

Cyndra rose. If no evil humors invaded the wound in his side, Sigestan should be hale within a fortnight. She prayed that would be so. Too many had died today.

"Sleep," she said softly, for others were already asleep on the crowded benches and on the floor of the great hall. She wished she could share their dreams, weaving a magic blanket of security which she would never know again.

A single brand burned over the table where her father consulted with the men who were not wounded. She knew what they were discussing. Manor Saeburgh had suffered a near fatal blow today, but the battle for England must not be lost upon this shore.

"Thank Brenwyn for me," Sigestan murmured, each word an effort.

Cyndra nodded. "We all are grateful to the men of Manor Darburgh for throwing their lot in with ours today."

"Thank *him.*"

"I will, but—"

He groped for her sleeve and drew her closer. "I never saw its like, Cyndra. There were a dozen Vikings on the hill. Brenwyn faced them alone. Each one he confronted lowered his sword and fled."

"How did you see that?"

"My eyes still worked." He tried to grin, but it became a wince. He folded her hand into a fist within his. "This, Cyndra, is the strength of Manor Saeburgh." He held up a single finger. "This was Brenwyn, alone against the Norse. What a fearsome reputation he must have! Do you think if Father makes him a thane, he will serve Manor Saeburgh?" He coughed and groaned. "We need him."

She drew a blanket over him. "Rest."

Inching through the tangle of bodies on the floor, she tried not to think how many corpses were unburied in the lower bailey. They could not afford to let more be killed simply to bury the dead. Dawn would be soon enough for the gruesome task.

Cyndra glanced at her father. The bandage around his head warned that a Viking blade had cut through his iron helmet. If he had died . . .

She lurched to the door. Below the last embers were hellish stars severing the darkness. The whisper of the sea broke the silence of death. The spirits of the dead were so broken they could not walk the night. It was as if the end of the world had come.

"How do you fare?" asked a deep voice.

She turned to smile at Brenwyn. Even in the faint light, his hair gleamed with raven fire. When he leaned one shoulder against the door frame, she wished she could rest her cheek on the other. "I will be glad when those who have died receive a decent grave."

"What will you do now?"

"What do you mean?"

"The fortress is destroyed. If they return—"

"Don't say that!"

He caught her by the shoulders. "They *will* come back, milady. You know that."

"You know much of Norse ways for a man who has lived far inland."

"How do you know that?"

Startled by his sudden venom, she frowned. "Mayhap I am mistaken, but I had thought Morcar wrote that his burgh had never been attacked by the Vikings."

He released his tight grip on her shoulders. "I have been at Manor Darburgh barely more than a year. Before that, I was well acquainted with Viking raids."

"You became the leader of Morcar's *fyrd* in such a short time?"

"Yes." He smiled.

Cyndra stared at him. Many warriors served for a lifetime without gaining that privileged rank. Her fingers settled on his arms. He had the strength of a warrior worthy of epic song, but she thought of his tenderness as he had held her while she wept until she learned Sigestan would survive.

She started to lean her head against his chest once more, then halted. One thing had not changed. He was a ceorl and she the daughter of an ealdorman. Nothing must exist between them but duty, respect, and obligation.

"So, you know we cannot flee," Cyndra whispered, staring out the door again. "We must rebuild. There are those who say that a burgh should be raised in stone like a church."

"Mayhap, but is there time for such an undertaking?" His hands on her arms brought her to face him. "A stone manor will take years to raise. Your father is hurt. Your brother has been wounded worse. Half of your father's *fyrd* is dead. The thane who led it lies among the dead below. You can no longer defend this shore."

She grasped his wrists. Raising his hands, she said, "These strong arms can help."

"Milady—"

"Heed me, Brenwyn. Pledge your sword to Father. He will grant you the lands and title you deserve. Thane Brenwyn."

"That has a pleasing sound, but it may be nothing more than your voice speaking my name."

"Brenwyn! I am serious."

"As I am." A smile played along his lips as he drew his arms away. "I thank you, milady, but I am pledged to serve Morcar at Manor Darburgh."

"We need you here. I saw what you—" She frowned at the bloodstains on his sleeve. "Has this been tended?"

"No, milady. It is nothing."

She pushed his sleeve up. He put out his hand to halt her, but she gasped in dismay at the gash on his arm. It still oozed blood. Tearing a strip from her ripped sleeve, she wrapped it around his forearm. Her fingers touched other puckered skin, but she ignored it. Any warrior as skilled as Brenwyn wore many scars.

"Have it looked at by Gleineth on the morrow," she said. "She knows how to watch for healing."

"And can she heal you, milady?"

"Heal me?"

His hand cupped her chin as his thumb brushed her cheek, being careful to avoid her bruised temple. She closed her eyes, relishing the delight she should not share with him.

"Is this the only injury you suffer?" he murmured.

"Thanks to you, it is."

Taking her right hand, he ran his finger along the small bandage she wore on her thumb. "And what of this?"

"I hurt it when I tried to open a chest. That accursed Viking took my keys! By all the saints! Now every chest will have to be broken open."

"Are these your keys?" He withdrew a ring from his pouch.

"How did you get these back?" She cradled the familiar keys before hooking them to the chain at her waist.

He smiled. "When I saw your girdle had been cut, I knew the warrior must have taken your keys. I offered him the chance to take another breath if he returned them to me. He saw the good sense of such a bargain."

"Please let my father reward you for your bravery."

"I would prefer a reward from you, milady." His mouth slanted across hers so quickly she could not react before he raised his head away. "A sweet reward, indeed, milady."

"It seems so little when you saved our lives." She could not keep the quiver from her voice. "Let Father—"

"I would rather you let *me,* pretty one."

His arm slipped around her waist, tugging her to him. As she gazed up into his glistening eyes, which promised so much, she knew he would not force her as the Viking would have. He was nothing like that beast. He was brave and honest . . . and everything she longed for in a protector. But she did not want to be protected right now. She wanted to escape, even for a single heartbeat, from the cruelty that had tortured her today and the overwhelming craving that had tormented her in her dreams.

Again he curved his finger under her chin, bringing it toward him. With a gentleness that sang within her heart, he explored her lips. Her fingers slid along his tunic and up into his silky hair as pleasure surged over her.

"Milady!" came a shocked gasp.

Cyndra turned to stare into Gleineth's wide eyes. "Yes?" Her voice quaked. When Brenwyn stroked her shoulder, she longed to lose herself in his luscious kisses.

"Your father wishes to see you." Gleineth frowned. "He wishes to see you immediately."

"Of course." She gathered her skirts in her hand. "Excuse me, Brenwyn."

Brenwyn nodded as Lady Cyndra rushed into the great hall. He fingered the bandage she had put on his wound and smiled. Tonight, Lady Cyndra's hair had been bound demurely beneath her veil, but he recalled its gold flowing along his arm on the hill. He wanted that splendor loosened once more across his bare skin as he leaned her beneath him.

He silenced his groan of frustration. Her father would as soon give her to a Viking as a ceorl in Morcar's service. Slowly his smile returned. She had asked him to become a thane in her father's *fyrd*. For a thane to possess an ealdorman's daughter was not unheard of.

No, that was impossible. Breaking Lady Cyndra's heart simply so he could enjoy her untasted charms was something he must not do. In his mind, he could hear his commander's derisive laughter. Had Brenwyn not learned to seize opportunity? To hesitate meant to lose it forever.

His jaw clenched as he silenced that taunting voice. Defeating an enemy was different from seducing this innocent woman who still believed that England could stop the Norse invasion. That courage of belief, misplaced though it might be, was something he had to admire.

But, curse his desires to the icy realms, he wanted more than a kiss from her.

Gleineth's whisper brought his attention back to her. "Even the ealdorman's gratitude, *Ceorl* Brenwyn, would not extend to allowing you to seduce his daughter."

He resisted laughing at the emphasis she put on his title. "Her kiss was nothing more than my reward for saving her from her father's enemies, who would have demanded far more."

She stepped closer so her full breasts brushed his arm. "An ealdorman's daughter may not be for you, but another woman could be." She walked her fingers up his arm. "My father was a ceorl, so my rank matches yours."

"You offer yourself so that your lady may not come to grief in her father's eyes?" He grinned wryly.

"Why pine for a woman you cannot have when there is one who would gladly share your blanket tonight?"

He shook his head. "Sleep is what awaits me tonight."

"If you fear you are betraying a woman at Manor Darburgh, it matters not when you remain at this manor."

"What makes you believe that?"

Gleineth scowled. "So, you will not accept the ealdorman's offer of service here?"

With a terse chuckle, he said, "It seems everyone

has heard of the honor Ealdorman Edgar intends to extend to me, save for me."

"Mayhap that is why he wishes to see you, too."

Brenwyn stood straighter. "Why did you say nothing of this before?"

"I wanted to speak with you alone so you might understand Lady Cyndra is not meant for you."

"Be assured, Gleineth, I know that."

Brenwyn strode toward the raised table. Edgar motioned for him to join him and Lady Cyndra on the platform. The ealdorman's advisors must have gone to check the watch.

Standing, the ealdorman put his hand on his daughter's shoulder. "I wish you to know I have made my decision."

"Decision, milord?" Even in the darkness, he could see the ealdorman's rigid mouth.

"You, Ceorl Brenwyn, and Morcar's men who survive will leave at dawn."

"As you wish, milord." He wondered who, besides Gleineth, had seen Lady Cyndra in his arms. He could imagine no other reason the ealdorman would banish him and his men.

Lady Cyndra stared at her father in disbelief. "Father, how can you send these men away? I had thought you would reward Brenwyn for—"

"Be silent, daughter."

Brenwyn fought not to scowl. Something else was amiss, something far more important than Lady Cyndra's kissing a ceorl.

"And you will take Cyndra with you." The ealdorman held out a rolled parchment. "You will escort her to Morcar. The betrothal agreement is signed."

"Father, you cannot mean that."

Edgar did not look at her. "I trust Morcar will abide by its provisions once he has married my daughter."

Brenwyn bit back his retort as Lady Cyndra dropped to her knees and seized her father's hand. Her face had no more color than the corpses in the lower bailey.

"Father, please—"

"Daughter, be silent."

She leaned her forehead against his hand. "Father, you pledged that you would allow me to decide whom I would wed. Oh, Father, please do not give me to Morcar."

The ealdorman's gaze locked with Brenwyn's. Could it be fear he saw in Edgar's eyes? Impossible! If the greatest foe of the Vikings quailed before their assaults, England was doomed. As the ealdorman bent to whisper to his daughter, Brenwyn glanced around the great hall. Mayhap, with his *fyrd* decimated and his burgh in ruins, even Edgar could not prevent the Norse conquest of England.

His hand clenched, and the parchment crushed in his grip. He understood what the ealdorman had not said. Ealdorman Edgar knew how small the chances were that Manor Saeburgh could survive another attack. Ealdorman Edgar believed that a marriage with Morcar of Manor Darburgh would be preferable for his daughter than having her become the thrall-mistress of a Viking.

But, Brenwyn knew with a pulse of horror, the ealdorman was wrong.

Four

Cyndra held her head high as Brenwyn brought forth her horse. Mayhap this way, the tears filling her eyes would not fall and embarrass her father.

Her gloved fingers clenched. Five armed men from her father's *fyrd* surrounded the pair of horses carrying the chests containing her dowry. Perched on a horse, Gleineth was wiping away tears. How Cyndra wished she could cry as openly. She must not.

Biting her lower lip, she fought to smile as Father came toward her. He kissed her cheek. "Go in peace, my daughter."

"I wish peace for all of us." She ached to grasp his arms and beg him to let her remain. Surely Father would come to his senses.

"My wish for you, child. Peace and a long, happy life."

"Will you send me tidings of Sigestan's recovery?"

Closing his eyes, he nodded. He took her hand and patted it. "I understand why you wished to remain by Sigestan's side until he awoke, but now the sun is nearly to its apex, and you have many leagues before you." He glanced to the sea. "You must travel with speed to reach Manor Darburgh before that storm reaches land."

Her throat burned with tears as he placed her hand in Brenwyn's. Looking from her father to Brenwyn, whose face could have been carved from the rocks along the shore, she swallowed roughly. This was the farewell she had believed would never come. Even a moment ago, she had dared to believe Father would change his mind and not force her to marry Thane Morcar.

"Guard my daughter with your life, Ceorl Brenwyn," Father said with quiet dignity, "until the hour Cyndra becomes the wife of Thane Morcar."

"I shall guard your blood with my life until that hour and beyond." He looked at the men who rode with him.

They dropped to one knee as Cerdic said, "We vow to guard your blood with our lives until that hour and beyond, milord."

Brenwyn smiled and bowed toward her father before capturing her gaze. She longed to lean her cheek against his chest as she had last night, seeking his comfort. No, she knew, as his thumb brushed her palm, it was not comfort that she wanted to share with him. She craved his mouth on hers as he tugged her to his strong chest.

Now, more than ever, such dreams were dead. With Father's signature on the betrothal contract, she belonged to Thane Morcar. By all the saints, this was wrong.

When Brenwyn lifted her onto her horse, Cyndra gripped the reins. She gazed around the ruined bailey at the faces she knew so well. Only Gleineth was going with her to Manor Darburgh. Gleineth and . . .

Brenwyn shouted an order. Cyndra turned her horse to follow his as he rode past the ravaged main gate of the manor. She did not look back, unable to endure the thought of seeing her father standing amid the ruins of what he had fought all his life to hold.

She flinched as she heard a shriek of grief. Death still stalked Manor Saeburgh, stealing those who could not survive their wounds.

When Brenwyn rode forward and grasped the reins of her horse, her grief flared into anger. "I am not a child! I have no need to have my horse led."

"It grows dark early among the trees." His answer was smooth and soothing. "My thane and your father directed me to safeguard you."

"Please grant me the dignity of riding without a lead."

He looked from her to the empty sea, then nodded. When he handed the leading rein back to her, his gloved fingers brushed hers. The thick leather between their skin seemed to vanish as a buzz, like a hive of bees, swarmed up her arm.

Brenwyn gave the order to ride toward the forest. When he glanced over his shoulder, she urged her mount forward. There was nothing else she could do, although she longed to race home. She halted her horse on a rise that gave her a last, clear view of the ocean.

Brenwyn stopped, too, but motioned for Cerdic to continue with the others along the narrow path. Without speaking, he watched as Cyndra gazed at the restless waters. Overhead the gray sky was quilted with clouds mirroring the waves.

His brow wrinkled in bafflement when she raised her hand as if to pluck the sea from its deep bed.

Her fingers clenched, and she drew them to her face. Closing her eyes, she relaxed her fingers so her palm was pressed to her lips. When her eyes reopened to look toward Ealdorman Edgar's burgh, he was not surprised to see jeweled tears on her lashes.

Cyndra did not flinch before his steady gaze. "I could hold back my tears when I said goodbye to Father and Sigestan, but to know that I shall never again look upon the sea—" She hid her face in her hands.

He moved his horse closer and turned her mount away from the sea. He put his finger under her chin, tilting it so she looked up into his face.

"Don't mourn," he whispered. "All you have loved is not gone. Look in your heart, and you'll find it there." He put a finger to the center of his chest. "I am far from the place of my birth, but I carry memories of it with me always."

"Give me a moment more."

"Milady, we must—"

"A moment more."

When he nodded reluctantly, she glanced over her shoulder and held out her hand. As she had before, she closed her fist and brought it back to her face.

"What are you doing?" he asked, unable to restrain his curiosity any longer.

A hint of a smile appeared on her quivering lips. "Don't think me witless, but I am taking a last breath of the sea air. I fear I will stifle without it."

"I like the sea best at sunrise when the waves are the same color as the sky, changing shades as the sun inches above the horizon." He sighed. "I see the sea so seldom now."

"You have lived near the sea?"

"I have, but now I live inland as you will. Surely you will welcome the safety of an inland burgh when the Vikings return."

Her eyebrows shot up as if propelled by a gust of wind. "I am no fool, Brenwyn. I know the sea is not the only route the Vikings choose for their attacks. They ride out of the Danelaw as well."

"Manor Darburgh is not an easy ride from the eastern holdings of the Danelaw." He frowned. "Your father sends you there to keep you safe, for he knows that you and every member of your family should seek a sanctuary."

"But he doesn't."

He put his hands over hers before she could swing her horse back toward Manor Saeburgh. His motion was as foolish as hers, he knew, when the craving gnawed at his gut once more. That need honed his voice. "Milady, do not be blind to the truth. Your father sends you to Morcar because he knows that he cannot serve the king to his best ability if he has to fear for you."

"I know." She looked back again.

"Your father is a wise man. He knows that Swein Forkbeard, the king of the Vikings, has carved himself an empire from the ruins of the world and he longs to add this island to it. Your father has been one of the reasons he has failed."

"So far."

He nodded. "So far, and your father wishes to keep Swein from claiming this land. If you wish to help him, you must obey him."

Her chin rose with pride. "It is my duty to help my father defend his lands as I can."

Brenwyn should not have been amazed, but he was. Even though she had nearly been raped and slain by the Vikings and her brother was still fighting for his life, she believed that her father would continue to defeat his foes. He could tell her that he— and her father—believed it was only a matter of time before the shoreline was overrun. But then he might have to tell her as well that her father should have given her the choice of dying in battle or being destroyed by Morcar's cruelty.

He turned his horse to follow the others before he spoke that truth . . . and how he was powerless to protect her against an enemy more vicious than any Viking.

Cyndra clung to her saddle as she swayed with the wind. Her body ached with each buffet. She was glad Brenwyn now held her horse's leading rein, because snow cut into her face each time she glanced up. The storm had swept down upon them an hour ago and showed no signs of abating. The journey had been uneventful for the past four days, but now they struggled the last league to Manor Darburgh.

Her face was taken in two gloved hands and turned toward Brenwyn's. His cheeks were coated with snow and the hoarfrost created by his breath.

"Release the reins, milady." The wind muted his words to a whisper.

Although puzzled, she tried to obey. Her fingers were too stiff to move. He peeled her left hand from the reins and held it between his hands as he captured her gaze. His fingers rose toward the mantle covering her lower face, but he drew them hastily away. Grasping her at the waist, he sat her on his lap.

"What do you think you are doing?" she cried.

"Mayhap saving your life. Your hands are half frozen."

"Brenwyn—"

"You are my thane's lady. I have vowed to protect you. Nothing you order will change my obligation. Sit still while I tie your horse's reins to mine." His voice gentled as he added, "Cerdic is helping Gleineth, to answer your next question."

When he held his cloak over her to shelter her from the storm, she leaned her face against his chest. Within the cocoon of his wool cape, she pulled aside her face mantle that had frozen. Brenwyn's iron-strong arm tightened around her, and she tried to ignore how his leg brushed hers, eliciting a now-forbidden delight. The steady beat of his heart beneath her ear was louder than the shriek of the wind.

"We don't have far to go, milady," he murmured.

"In this weather, I doubt we could go far. It . . ." Her gaze was held by his intense eyes. The screech of the wind and the crash of the branches vanished.

His gloved hand curved along her cheek. "You now belong to Morcar, but I find it most difficult to remember that as I hold you in my arms."

She stiffened. "To speak as you do is improper."

"Improper?" His laugh chilled her more. His hand swept up her back to press her closer. Fury glittered in his eyes more brightly than the freshly falling snow. In a low growl, he said, "You have yet to learn what is improper, milady. When your husband returns to bed you, you shall learn what is improper."

"By every saint, I said that was enough, Ceorl Brenwyn!"

He recoiled at her words. She wanted to apologize, but must not. She was his thane's lady.

They rode in silence. Sorrow choked her. He had overstepped himself . . . as she had wanted him to. Her yearning to taste his kiss refused to be lessened simply because her father had signed a betrothal contract with Thane Morcar.

When his hand rubbed her back, his compassion teased her to throw caution aside. She looked up at his stern face. "I should not have spoken like that, Brenwyn."

"Cyndra," he answered, using her name without her title with an ease that astonished her, "you were correct. I presume too much with my thane's lady. I am a ceorl. I should not dream of holding you close to my heart so I might feel yours racing like the wind as I bring your lips to mine."

She shook her head. His words turned her blood into liquid fire. "Do not speak so!"

"Forgive me, milady. I have no wish to bring you unhappiness. I must forget my longing to taste your sweet lips, which are more luscious than the first berries of summer."

His arm tightened around her again as his mouth lowered toward hers, contradicting his words and offering her what she wanted. She closed her eyes, splaying her fingers across his broad chest. Beneath her touch, his heartbeat leaped to echo hers. She wanted this pleasure—just once more.

"Brenwyn!" came a shout.

Cyndra pulled away. Brenwyn caught her before she could slip off his lap.

Flashing her a regretful smile, he called, "What is it, Cerdic? This wind is deafening."

She made sure her face was blank when Cerdic drew even with them.

"We are on the hill above Manor Darburgh, Brenwyn," he shouted. "You told us to stop here so the ladies could ride into the manor on their own horses if they wished."

Brenwyn returned to the formality he had forsaken when he drew her against him. "Milady, do you wish to resume your seat on your horse?"

Cyndra turned to Gleineth, who sat behind Cerdic. "What is your wish?"

"Whatever you decide is fine with me." Gleineth's words were distorted by her shivering lips.

"We shall stay as we are." She saw relief in her maid's eyes.

As Brenwyn shouted orders to his men, he winked boldly. To the others, she might be able to pretend her concern was for Gleineth, but he knew the truth. Leaning against him as the horses began down the steep hill, she enjoyed the last opportunity she had to be in his arms.

"Look and see if you can catch a glimpse of Manor Darburgh," he whispered against the hood of her cloak.

Cyndra strained to see through the storm. Suddenly a dark hulk appeared through the curtain of snow.

The walls of the burgh had been constructed of tree trunks strengthened by earthworks. The gate was only wide enough for two horsemen to ride through side by side. The burgh should be able to withstand invaders or resist a siege aimed at it.

"Who goes?" came a shout.

Brenwyn called back what she guessed was a password. The double doors in the gate swung open.

A flutter twisted in her stomach. This would be her home for as long as she was married to Morcar. She almost begged Brenwyn to turn the horse about and take her back to Manor Saeburgh. She could not. Father had sent her here. She must do her duty to her family and to him.

Brands fought back the darkness. A half-dozen men surrounded the horses. Inquisitive glances focused on her, and she was grateful for her cloak as Brenwyn helped her from the horse. When he released her and turned to help Gleineth, the fear returned doubly strong. She was sure she had never been so alone . . . and so scared.

A door opened in one of the shadows that must be buildings. She frowned. If this was Manor Darburgh's great hall, it was not raised far above the bailey. Mayhap Thane Morcar did not believe his hall should be raised high as a sanctuary and a place for the *fyrd* to fire down on invaders. If so, he was a fool. No place in England was safe now.

She peered through the snow to count the number of burs scattered around the bailey. Each provided private quarters for a thane or trusted ceorl. The small buildings had room for a bed, a servant's pallet, and little else. Manor Darburgh was so different from Manor Saeburgh, where most of the residents lived within the comfort of the great tower.

"Milady, I believe that is your bur." Gleineth pointed at a building to the left of the main hall. "It is quite large."

Brenwyn cleared his throat. "That is the thane's private bur. By Thane Morcar's orders, the second largest bur has been set aside for you."

"He has quarters private from his wife?" Cyndra wished she had not spoken when she saw Brenwyn's eyes narrow. Why did Morcar, who had wanted to marry her to obtain an heir, wish to keep his own bur? She wanted to ask Brenwyn to explain, but could not when so many ears waited to hear every word.

As they climbed the trio of steps to the door of the great hall, Brenwyn held his cloak over her shoulders. "Here is your grand hall, milady."

She flinched at the sarcasm in his voice. His low opinion of his thane and this burgh worried her. If he hated it here, why did he stay? She could not ask that question now, either.

Cyndra was swept away from Brenwyn as the ceorls' ladies joyously welcomed her. They brought her near the fire pit in the center of the hall. She threw back her cloak to relish the heat.

As each person was introduced to her with the greatest formality, Cyndra urged, "Do not curtsy to me tonight."

The women exchanged worried glances.

"My fingers are frozen from the ride." With a smile, she added, "Please give them a chance to thaw." She pulled off her gloves and tried to flex her stiff hands, hoping they would understand that she could not signal them to come to their feet again.

As she chafed her fingers, she looked about the hall. It could have fit into the kitchens of Manor Saeburgh. Hearing birds scratching overhead, she looked at the rafters, where heavy battle banners hung. She grimaced when she saw nests. No doubt, there would be other vermin, too. That must change.

Quietly, she asked, "Do you feed the whole burgh here?"

A woman who was nearly as round as the fire pit answered, "With Thane Morcar and his thanes away, there are no more than a score plus ten eating here."

"So few?" Cyndra could not hide her surprise. Over one hundred people lived in her father's manor . . . or had lived there before the Vikings' attack. "And do you have plenty of livestock to provide meat and eggs?"

Brenwyn accepted a cup of heated mead as he eavesdropped on Cyndra's first meeting with her household. When he heard her insightful questions, he hid his smile behind his drinking horn. She would do well. His lips tightened. She would do well *until* Morcar returned. Then her life would become the hell they all knew too well.

He wanted to curse Ealdorman Edgar for failing to see the truth. It was too late now. Now it was *his* duty to try to protect Cyndra.

As long as he could.

He turned to his men for a report. As he expected, things had been quiet. Very seldom was there any trouble when Morcar and his thanes were gone. When they returned, the baiting of the ceorls would begin anew. Even though Brenwyn cautioned his men to ignore the insults, eventually someone would react. Then violence would erupt.

Brenwyn sighed. If the ceorl won, the man would pay with his life for daring to slay a thane. If the thane won, the cruelty grew more intense. Morcar did not care that a ceorl died. The thane was concerned only with his pleasures.

Now a new pawn had been added to this game. Brenwyn had not been here when Morcar brought his previous wife home, but he had heard tales of what that lady had endured. She had succumbed to death less than three months after the wedding. Outside the manor, it was said she had died of a fever. Within, it was whispered she had killed herself to escape Morcar. Now the thane would have Cyndra.

His gaze strayed to where she was removing her cloak. Her blue gown followed her enticing form before tumbling to trail behind her on the floor. Over it she wore a burgundy, knee-length tunic. Her hair was completely hidden by her veil that was edged with gold embroidery.

Listening to her melodic voice, he swallowed his sorrow when he thought of her innocence being driven from her by Morcar's bestiality. Even worse was knowing how powerless he was to halt Morcar from demanding anything he wished from his new wife. He snarled his grandfather's favorite curse under his breath.

Cyndra kept her eyes averted from Brenwyn's gaze. As she greeted the women, who were vying to impress her, every sense was attuned to him. She waited for the sound of his laugh and his words.

When her stomach grumbled, she blushed.

"You have not eaten, milady?" asked a woman who had been eyeing her clothes with undisguised envy.

Cyndra marked her as a source of trouble. Jealousy could rip apart a hall as completely as an enemy attack. "Not since morning."

The women rushed to bring the bowls and drinking horns to the tables. When Cyndra sat at a table by the fire pit instead of the raised table at the far end of the room, they again exchanged uneasy glances. She did not care. She wanted to stay here where it was warm . . . and there was a chance Brenwyn might sit nearby.

Midway through the meal, silence settled on the hall. A woman stood and held out the household keys. "As our men pledge their service to Thane Morcar, Lady Cyndra, so do the women vow to do as you command."

"As the thane offers protection to those who follow him, so shall I succor in times of sickness or need all who reside within my hall," she replied correctly. She smiled when she attached the ring of iron keys to her belt. To marry and have the soft sound of clanking keys by her side was a woman's grandest achievement. So Father had said often. But he had been false when he said she could select her husband. What other lies had he told her?

Tears filled her eyes. Father had his reasons for sending her here. Yet, she would rather have died fighting for Manor Saeburgh than be wedded to Thane Morcar, whose name brought only expressions of disdain from those who should be his allies.

Brenwyn stood, his frown warning that her thoughts might have been visible for all to see. Or were only *his* eyes clear enough to see the truth?

"Milady, if you and Gleineth wish to retire after our long journey, I would show you to your bur," he said.

"We would appreciate that," Cyndra answered as she saw Gleineth struggling to stay awake. That her maid was not flirting with the men in the great hall should have warned her that Gleineth was exhausted. The fire's heat after the day's chill was as soothing as a lullaby. As she rose, the household came to their feet, shocking her. Father did not require such obeisance. "Gleineth?"

"Thank you, milady," the redhead said when Cyndra took her arm to help her stand.

The cold stole Cyndra's breath as they crossed the bailey. Snow drifted lazily from the charcoal sky. Near the wall, torches burned to let the sentries see into the night. A strange silence had settled on the burgh. Or, Cyndra had to admit, she hoped it was an odd silence. At Manor Saeburgh, she had been surrounded by noises from the kitchen and the stables and her family.

Opening the door of the bur that would be hers, she was pleased the lamp had been lit and a fire was burning on the open hearth. The hall needed so much work, but the bur was almost perfect.

Next to the hearth, that reached its stone claws out onto the wooden floor, was a bench. A cupboard bed was built into the opposite wall. Its doors could be closed during the day. A painted chest was the only other piece of furniture other than a small cot for Gleineth's use behind a curtain.

"Thank you, Brenwyn," Gleineth said.

Cyndra turned. Brenwyn's skin sparkled with the snow that had fallen during their short walk from the hall. When her gaze was caught by his, her breath clogged in her throat. The warmth of his eyes reached within her to melt her trepidation when she thought of how Thane Morcar had had three previous wives who had lived here before her.

"Thank you, Brenwyn," she whispered, "for escorting us to our bur." She wished she could say how pleased she was that she could depend on him in this strange place. She wished she could tell him how desperately she wanted his arms around her.

"It has been my privilege to bring you to Manor

Darburgh," he replied, but she suspected he was lying to her. He dropped to his knees.

"No, Brenwyn! Don't kneel to me!" Her hands were curving around his face before she realized what she was doing. Her fingers snapped back as if fire had seared them.

When he looked past her, she saw Gleineth regarding her with dismay.

Cyndra's laugh sounded stilted, even to her ears. "I know you must be as brittle from the long, cold ride as we are."

"You are thoughtful, milady, but a warrior grows accustomed to a hard life. I would be honored to show you about Manor Darburgh tomorrow after I drill the *fyrd* on their daily exercises."

"Until the morrow, then."

"Good evening, Lady Cyndra, Gleineth." As he dipped his head, Brenwyn saw unease on the redhead's face. She continued to fear he would compromise her lady.

He almost laughed, thinking of the restraint he had shown when he had held Cyndra on the horse. Did Gleineth—or Cyndra—know how he had longed to slip away into the storm and find a shelter where he could teach her to release the passion that was hinted in her kiss?

Going out into the night, he held his face up to the cleansing air. The snow was changing to sleet and cut into his skin. He needed the sharp sting to help him regain his perspective.

He was bound to serve at Manor Darburgh by an oath. For almost a year, he had worked with the *fyrd* and gained respect within Manor Darburgh and beyond its walls. He could not throw aside all he had worked for in exchange for Cyndra's kisses.

Bowing his head to the storm, he strode toward the stables. There, he had his own corner. Although Brenwyn was commander of the *fyrd,* Morcar had not given him a private bur. It was another insult, like the insult of leaving Brenwyn behind while Morcar went to pay court on King Ethelred.

Brenwyn chuckled. If Morcar had known how pleased he was to remain here, Morcar would have insisted he go to East Anglia. This situation suited Brenwyn perfectly. It had been perfect, he amended, until Ealdorman Edgar signed that betrothal contract, giving Cyndra to Morcar.

With a sigh, he entered the stable that smelled of sweat and animals. He sought out his pallet. It was separated from the stalls by a curtain like the one in Cyndra's bur. He cursed. He could not get Cyndra from his mind.

He sat on his pallet, folding his arms on his knees and leaning his head on them. If he were wise, he would erase every thought of lovely Lady Cyndra from his brain before his desire for her destroyed both of them. He wondered if that were possible. It must be, or everything he had endured here would be for naught.

Five

Cyndra watched as the servants whirled about the floor gaily. Beneath her gown, her toes tapped in tempo with the music. Traveling minstrels had stopped for the night and were exchanging their music for a place to sleep. A pipe, a lap harp, and a drum created cheerful tunes. Although she longed to dance, it would not be wise for her to ask a ceorl. That might start whispers of favorites that could create trouble in this uneasy burgh where rank seemed to be more important than anything else.

With a satisfied sigh, she looked about the great hall. For the past fortnight, she had taught the servants to meet her standards of cleanliness. Now, even the rafters were free of filth.

Her days were full as she supervised the kitchens and the hall. Staying busy offered her a refuge. A week after her arrival, she had received a brusque message from Thane Morcar. It had informed her he would not be returning to Manor Darburgh for at least another fortnight. When she read "I have more important matters to tend to than paying court on you," she pretended the words did not hurt.

She dreaded Thane Morcar's return. Unguarded comments among the ceorls warned her that Bren-

wyn was not the only one who had no respect for
the thane. Many of the ceorls feared Thane Morcar.

Looking across the crowded room as the pipe
trilled, Cyndra saw Brenwyn laughing with his men.
He seemed unaware of her as her gaze slipped from
his smile, past the stern line of his jaw, and along
the firm muscles beneath his dark-green tunic. Since
her arrival here, she had seen him seldom. Spring
brought more need to train Thane Morcar's *fyrd*, so
he spent most days riding about the countryside
with his men from before dawn until after she fell
asleep. A pang pricked her when she realized she
could not remember the last time she had spoken
more than a greeting to him as they passed in the
bailey.

"Milady?"

Looking up hopefully, although she knew the
voice was too high for Brenwyn's, Cyndra managed
to smile as Cerdic bowed his head. "Good evening,
Cerdic."

"Milady, would you consider honoring a clumsy
ceorl with a dance?"

She laughed. "I have watched you. You do yourself
an injustice to call yourself *clumsy.*"

"I shall endeavor to keep your feet from my awk-
ward ones."

Smiling, she took his hand. He led her to the middle of the floor and swirled her into the dance. The
pattern was infinitely changing. He colored like a
child when his toe came down on hers, but she
chuckled.

"Forgive me for not keeping my vow, milady," he
said with a smile as the song ended.

"He *is* a most dangerous man when dancing,"
came a warm voice from behind her.

Cyndra took a slow breath to steady her heartbeat. Thanking Cerdic, she faced Brenwyn. He dipped in a quick obeisance, and she bit back the joy she wanted to shout. She must not tell him that he was too often a part of her dreams, even though too seldom a part of her day.

"Would you like to dance with me, Cyndra?" he asked so lowly that she alone could hear him use her given name.

He held out his hand, and she put hers in it. A quiver sliced through her, leaving bare her longings. His broad fingers entwined with hers as he drew her a single step closer.

"I am afraid I delayed too long," he said with a laugh. He pointed toward where the minstrels were putting away their instruments.

"Then I must bid you thank you and good night." She struggled to smile.

"The music is over, but the evening need not be."

"I must—"

"Go for a walk with me, for I have something I wish to share with you."

Heat climbed her cheeks. "Brenwyn, do not speak so!"

"I do not, not of what you clearly are imagining." He laughed as he motioned toward the door. "I am suggesting only a walk."

"It must be a short one." She was risking trouble, but she could not resist this chance to be with him.

The balmy evening welcomed them in the moonlight. A breeze played with her veil, twisting it about her shoulders as she walked with him toward the back of the burgh. Pungent smells came from the byres. When they had left the glow from the hall behind them, he took her hand once more.

"Brenwyn, I swear by all the saints that you dare much." She looked down as he laced his fingers through hers.

"I keep you close to protect you from the dangers of the night."

"And who shall protect me from your foolishness?"

He smiled. "Is it more foolish than avoiding you during this past fortnight because I cannot trust myself not to touch you even this chastely?"

"That is not foolish. That is mad." She pulled away.

Catching her arm, he urged, "Cyndra, we must talk."

"We have nothing to talk of when there can be nothing between us."

"At least, come with me to see what I wish to show you." His fingers softened to stroke her arm.

Quivers coursed along her, spiraling outward from his fingers. "Yes," she heard herself say, fearing she was mad. When he did not take her hand as they continued, she fought not to slip her fingers through his. "I have a request of you."

"You know you need only to ask."

The soft roughness in his voice urged her to say something different, but she answered, "Please let me know before you promote one of your men."

"You want to run the *fyrd* and the hall, milady?" He laughed. "I know from the wound you inflicted on your enemy's arm that you would be a stalwart warrior."

"I have no interest in overseeing your *fyrd*." She did not want to speak of the Vikings' attack that had ended with her banishment here. "Didn't you realize that when you made Ecgbert a subcaptain, his wife gained status as well? Many of the ceorls are not pleased that Hild now holds a higher rank."

Brenwyn chuckled at her grimace. "Hild has longed to gain your favor, milady."

"She will not when she disrupts everything in the hall."

"Ecgbert is an excellent warrior."

"I know that must be so." She sighed. "I will deal with Hild."

"You have been busy, milady, with your domestic trials." As he had been busy with thoughts of her. The combination of her loveliness, that created a fire like an ulcer in his gut, and her capable handling of any crisis had convinced him that he must be alone with her. He had battled this yearning. Every day, it had grown stronger as he imagined her in his arms.

"I swear one of these days, we shall find Hild with a knife in her ribs," she said, her soft words weaving through his fantasies.

"Yours?"

He expected her to laugh, but her voice became grim. "I prefer to save my blade for Norse blood."

"Then I shall leave this problem to you and your household," he replied with a forced chuckle. He cursed silently. She never forgot the threat of attack. Neither had he, until tonight when he could think only of her lips. "I am sure you will settle this with skill, as you have everything else in the past two weeks."

"Two weeks? It seems I have been at Manor Darburgh for a lifetime."

"I can understand that. You have done a lifetime of work and created magic, milady."

"Magic?"

"I have never seen the people here so productive or so happy."

"I am pleased with them. They have learned what I require so well it seems they can read my thoughts."

He tilted her face up so he could see her delicate features in the scant light. "It is fortunate no one can guess my thoughts."

She drew away from him again. "It is late, Brenwyn. If you wish to show me this surprise—"

"Tonight, share your delightful company with me. Although I wish it could be far more, milady, I will acquiesce to your wishes."

"Is that a vow?"

With a smile, he shook his head. "Unlike Cerdic, who broke his pledge not to step on your toes, I will make no vows I may be unable to keep."

"Do you wish me to believe I was in more danger from Cerdic than I am from you?"

"I shall never do anything to hurt you." When her eyes widened, he added, "Come, and I shall show you this surprise."

Cyndra said nothing as Brenwyn led her past the sheepfold. She paused to look over the fence at the lambs. Their soft *baas* were ignored by the ewes.

She knelt and put her fingers through the fence. Her hands swept along the lambs' tightly curled hair. As the lambs ran away, she stood and rubbed her palms together.

Brenwyn ran his finger across her palm. His smile was shadowed by the night, but she could hear his amusement. "Is this a woman's secret? Touch a sheep before allowing a man to touch you, so your skin is soft."

She laughed. "You must know that women use

sheep's wool for their skin for the same reason warriors use it to keep leather supple."

"You make it difficult to compliment you." He motioned toward the stable. "My surprise is this way."

"No hints?"

Smiling, he said, "Only that you will be pleased with it."

The shadowed stable was hushed. She followed Brenwyn to the stall where a mare stood guard on a newborn colt.

"He's beautiful," she murmured, not wanting to rouse any of the ceorls who were asleep on their pallets.

"A warhorse bred strong and fast." Pride warmed his voice. "His sire is Morning Fire."

"Your horse?"

"I should not be surprised that you know the name of my mount." He smiled as he folded his arms on the stall.

Looking back at the foal, she asked, "What do you intend to do with him?"

"Me? The colt is Thane Morcar's, milady." He took her arm and led her out of the stable. "All of the horses belong to him. The ceorls ride only on his favor. I brought Morning Fire with me to Manor Darburgh, but now he is Thane Morcar's, as I am, with my oath of allegiance."

"If you left—"

"Morning Fire would go with me as does my sword." He chuckled. "Of course, the truth is that Morning Fire has allowed no other man on his back since I began riding him."

Cyndra crossed her arms in front of her. The night seemed to have lost its warmth. "I do not understand why Thane Morcar would want to lay claim to all these steeds."

"Greed, milady." His voice grew hard. "What is Thane Morcar's, he shares with no other. What is not his, he impoverishes himself to obtain."

Cyndra gasped as she realized what he meant.

"I apologize, milady, to speak so of your betrothed. I know Ealdorman Edgar wants only the best for you. It is unfortunate that he decided that the best was Thane Morcar."

"Don't say that."

"I have no wish to be false with you."

"Can we speak of something else?"

His hands framed her cheeks. "Shall we speak of how your face would not grow taut with terror if you were not beginning to learn the truth of the demon who holds Manor Darburgh?"

Closing her eyes, she put her hands over his. She drew them away, although she ached for his touch. "Rather you should tell me good night."

"I would rather do something other than *tell* you good night."

Before she could answer, his mouth captured hers. His arms slipped around her to bring her against him. His leg brushed hers, setting her skin afire. As his lips wove a path of pleasure along her face, he pressed her against the wall of the stable. The caress of him along her vanquished all other thoughts. His fingers explored her with eager delight. Hearing her breath rasping rapidly, she steered his mouth back to hers. She wanted to savor the fire of his kisses.

Madness! shouted her mind, but she ignored the warning as his hand grazed her breast and she moaned. The sensation was so sweet, she feared she would succumb to its pleasure.

When he whispered her name against her veil, Cyndra pushed herself out of his arms and stumbled toward the kitchen. He halted her, but his hand was as tender as his lips had been. His face was dappled by the starlight filtering through the unfurling leaves.

"I beg your forgiveness again," he whispered. "I do not want you to be unhappy tonight, milady. Who knows when I shall be able to hold you so again?"

Her fingers caressed his rough cheek. "It must be never."

"That I do not want to admit."

"But we must."

He started to reply, but paused as the cry of an owl severed the night. She was unsure if he smiled or if it were a trick of the faint light. Bending, he kissed her cheek. "What *you* must do is go back to your bur, milady."

"Now?" If he had told her that he had been crowned king, she would have been no more surprised by his sudden change of heart.

"Now." His tone suggested that he would accept no disagreement.

As they crossed the empty bailey, he took her hand. He squeezed her fingers at the door of her bur, but said nothing as he slipped away into the shadows.

She leaned her head against the door, unwilling to go in and put an end to this night's rapture. But it was over. It had been the moment Father signed the betrothal contract. Thane Morcar would be her husband, even though she was falling in love with one of his ceorls.

Six

A knock sounded on the door of Cyndra's bur. Gleineth hurried to open it.

"I wish to speak to Lady Cyndra," Brenwyn said in a stern tone, "of news arriving at the gate."

Looking up from where she had been adding embroidery to the hem of her dress, Cyndra started to smile. It faded as foreboding sank her stomach. His hooded eyes allowed no hint of what he was thinking.

Gleineth whispered, "Milady, if you will excuse me, I shall get that length of material you wish from the hall."

"Yes." Pulling the key ring from her belt, she handed it to her maid. Her gaze remained on Brenwyn's face as Gleineth scurried away. "Brenwyn, what is wrong?"

He stepped into her bur, making it seem so much smaller. He did not close the door. "A message has come from the entourage of Thane Morcar. He shall return to Manor Darburgh by nightfall."

"Thane Morcar?" Her hand rose to her mouth as she stared at her needlework. She had been a fool to lose herself in the dream that Brenwyn was the man she would wed. Now Thane Morcar was returning, a man despised by his ceorls and rumored to be a coward whose word had no value.

The door closed softly. She gasped. She did not want to be alone with her fear.

"Cyndra?" whispered Brenwyn.

She looked up. She was not alone. With a moan, she threw her arms around him. He stroked her back as she whispered against his tunic, "I don't want him to come back."

"Calm yourself, Cyndra." His fingers curved around her face. His pain-darkened eyes held hers. "You asked me last night if I would make a vow to you."

"By every saint, you know that there can be no vows between us when I am obligated to Morcar."

"I vow I will do all I can to keep you from being hurt, milady."

"I know." Stepping away, she wrapped her arms around herself, for Brenwyn's arms could offer her a haven no longer.

"I cannot stay. The news of Morcar's return is spreading through the burgh, so Gleineth will be hurrying back to prepare you to meet your husband." When she flinched, he put his hands on her shoulders and whispered, "Be strong, Cyndra."

"I am the daughter of Ealdorman Edgar of Manor Saeburgh. I will not shame my father."

His sorrowful smile told her he knew that, no matter how she pretended, she dreaded meeting Thane Morcar. "Your father shall be proud of you, Cyndra." His fingers lingered against her cheek. "As I am."

Cyndra stared as he left. Her heart begged her to race after him and devise a deranged plan to flee this place. She sighed. Her father's signature on the

marriage contract obligated her to marry Thane
Morcar of Manor Darburgh.

Gleineth burst into the bur with the news of Thane
Morcar's impending arrival. The words washed over
Cyndra as her maid chose the gown Cyndra would
wear to meet Morcar. She dressed in a dark-green
dress with its paler overtunic. As Gleineth brushed
her hair and swirled it into a pattern about her head,
Cyndra tried to think of nothing. Again and again
the image of Brenwyn tried to form, but she forced
it away.

A ceorl knocked on the door. Wringing her dress,
the young woman announced, "Milady, Thane Morcar's party has been sighted."

"Thank you," Cyndra answered, wondering how
she could sound so calm.

Gleineth readjusted Cyndra's veil. "You need not
be nervous, milady. Thane Morcar has expressed a
great desire to have you for his bride. Such a longing
will make him eager to please you."

"Or for me to please him," she whispered under
her breath as she led Gleineth to the great hall.

Along the walls, the ceorls stood in silence as Cyndra walked with Gleineth into the hall. She was stepping up next to the raised table when she heard the
horn announcing the return of the thanes to the
manor. She paid no attention to Gleineth arranging
her gown to be most flattering. At her sides, her
clammy hands clenched in her long sleeves.

The doors were opened wide. From across the
empty floor, her gaze was caught and held by Brenwyn, who entered amid a crowd of strangers.

As they neared, she squared her shoulders. Not
for a moment could she allow herself to forget that

she was the daughter of Ealdorman Edgar. She would make her father proud of her.

She must.

Brenwyn stepped forward, but turned his back on her. The motion, more than anything else, warned her that she must be subservient to the thane. She looked at the men he faced. They were filthy from their travels. Which one was her future husband?

"Milord, by your leave," said Brenwyn without emotion, "I would present to you Lady Cyndra. Milady, by your leave, I would present to you Thane Morcar of Manor Darburgh."

When Brenwyn pointed to a man directly in front of him, Cyndra was grateful for the long hours of training on how to conceal her opinions. Otherwise, her distress would have been displayed for all to see. Until now, the two decades difference in hers and Thane Morcar's ages had not seemed dramatic. Her father was more than thirty years her senior, but his active life gave him firm muscles and a sharp mind.

Thane Morcar was not like her father. His hair was streaked with gray and his features, pinched with avarice. His body was layered with excess flesh. When he stepped forward, he took her hand and drew her down beside him. Disgust wafted along her spine at his sweaty touch.

"My dear lady," he said, "I would have you stand next to me, not above me."

"That is where a wife should be." She met his narrowed eyes and understood that she must never remind him of her higher status again.

"I have waited long to be with you. 'Twas only the demands of my king that have kept me from your side."

Cyndra wanted to shout that his words were lies.

The harsh words of his single missive were etched into her heart, but she said, "You do me honor, milord."

A man by Morcar's side cleared his throat. He was a handsome man, although not as broad in the shoulder as Brenwyn. His hair was dark and his clothes of the finest cut. His expression warned that he found this meeting amusing.

Morcar said, "Milady, this is my chief thane, Athelbert."

Athelbert bowed. "I am honored, milady, to be present at this joyous occasion."

Dipping her head, she said, "Rise, Thane Athelbert. Thank you for your gracious welcome."

"You see, my friend," Morcar said, "she is a most delightful creature."

"I think she will be a proper match for you, milord."

Cyndra watched as her betrothed preened, then she asked, "Do you wish to relax after your long journey?"

"Yes, milady. Come here." With a laugh, he gripped her chin and twisted her mouth beneath his.

When he ran his hands along her, she could not contain her quivers of fear. The closeness which had been so sweet with Brenwyn was sickening with the one man who had the right to touch her. She pushed against his chest. "Milord, this is most undignified." Her words sounded silly, but she would say anything to escape.

"So shy, Cyndra?" He chuckled as he turned her face so he could view it from every angle. "Your maidenly ways speak well of your upbringing, but a man tires of such virtue." He laughed again as he steered her reluctant mouth beneath his.

Brenwyn watched Morcar avidly kissing Cyndra. He kept his face blank and hoped his eyes did not reveal his rage. *Rage and jealousy.* The memory of Cyndra's sweet lips haunted him. When she clenched her fists as Morcar wrapped his arms around her, Brenwyn took a half-step forward.

"No, my friend," whispered Cerdic.

Brenwyn nodded, his jaw tightening. Every curse he knew rang through his head. He wanted to draw his sword and fight his way to Cyndra and take her from Manor Darburgh. That he must not do. Even if other obligations did not restrain him, he would not risk her life. Morcar must never suspect that he had not been the first to taste Cyndra's lips.

Morcar did not release Cyndra as he faced Brenwyn. "Send for the priest. Milady and I will not spend another night apart."

"Father Augustine is not here."

"Not here?"

"He has been called away by the bishop for some meeting."

With a curse, he snarled, "Then send to another burgh."

Brenwyn was careful not to look at Cyndra, for he doubted if he could keep from smiling if he saw the relief that must be on her face. "I shall, milord; but, with nightfall imminent, the priest will not be here before late on the morrow."

When Morcar bellowed another curse, Cyndra edged away and motioned for mead to be served to the thane and his men. He whirled to glare at her, then smiled as a jeweled goblet was thrust into his hand.

Morcar held it high. "To my beautiful Lady Cyndra!" he crowed. "May she bring me dozens of legitimate sons!"

"And much pleasure," Athelbert added.

Brenwyn did not drink to the toast and noted the halfhearted reaction from the other ceorls. Those who had come to admire their lady did not want her in Morcar's bed.

Morcar called, "Brenwyn, come forward."

Brenwyn walked to where Morcar now sat at the center of the raised table. He glanced at Cyndra, who stood beside her betrothed. Her face was blank, but despair dimmed her eyes.

"Do you forget yourself, Brenwyn?" Morcar drawled. He smiled as Athelbert snickered.

Sinking to his knees, Brenwyn lowered his head so he did not have to see Cyndra's horror. Few thanes required such deference from their own ceorls, but Morcar wanted to humiliate him.

"It appears," continued Morcar, "that you have proven your value to me, once again, by bringing milady safely to Manor Darburgh."

"You are most gracious, my thane."

Morcar loosened his cape and dropped it over the back of his chair. "Rise, Brenwyn. You are dismissed. Be prepared to report on matters of the manor tomorrow before the wedding."

He heard the mutter of dismay from his men. They were angry to see the commander of the *fyrd* treated with so little respect and remain unrewarded for his fidelity.

"Thane Morcar—" Cyndra began.

"Go, and arrange for our evening meal, my lovely lady," Morcar ordered.

She dipped in the merest of curtsies. "As you wish,

milord," she murmured. Without looking back, she left the hall with Gleineth trailing her like a shadow.

Brenwyn called out the order for the men to finish their day's training. The time was coming when they would have to fight. They must be prepared. He glanced toward Cyndra's bur as he walked out of the hall. Yes, they must be prepared. All of them.

Cyndra waited until she saw Brenwyn come back into the burgh after setting his men to their drills. Pushing herself away from the window, she said, "Gleineth, I must check on preparations in the kitchen."

The redhead shivered. "Milady, do you think that is wise? Mayhap, you should stay here away from—"

"Thane Morcar—"

"I do not speak of him, but of Brenwyn."

"He is suffering because of me!"

"He will suffer more if Thane Morcar discovers how you pine for his ceorl."

"Gleineth!"

"I speak the truth." Gleineth looked down at her hands. "I thought once he might turn his eye to me, but all his thoughts have been of you since he arrived at Manor Saeburgh." Raising her gaze, she whispered, "The thane would see Brenwyn slain most torturously if he guessed the truth, and no man would cry *nay.*"

"I know that." She glanced at the door.

"Go, if you must. Go, but remember your place and his."

"How can I forget? Tomorrow I must marry Morcar. After tomorrow, I must think only of Morcar."

"Can you?"

"I must try." She rushed out of the bur, but slowed so no one would think anything was amiss. She wondered why she tried to maintain this delusion. Everyone in Manor Darburgh knew nothing was the same.

Cyndra hoped their meeting appeared casual as she greeted Brenwyn. "I wanted to check with the kitchen," she repeated her lame lie.

"I think you shall find everything as you wish." He glanced at the hall, then said, "I would be honored to show you a new foal in the stables, milady."

"Another?"

"One new foal."

She frowned, then realized this was his way of talking to her . . . alone. She wanted nothing more. "I would appreciate that. Do you have the time now?" She struggled not to look around to see if anyone was watching.

"Now would be convenient, milady."

Cyndra wished she had an excuse to touch Brenwyn as they walked into the empty barn. Without pausing to look at the colt, he seized her hand and drew her behind a curtain. She frowned as she looked at the rolled pallet beside an unadorned chest.

"What is this place?" she asked.

"My quarters, milady."

"This? You are the commander of the *fyrd*."

He laughed mirthlessly. "A post that Morcar holds in little esteem."

"You keep this manor ready and train his *fyrd*. Yet he treats you with less respect than he would a slave."

Sitting on the chest, he took her hand between his. He drew her down next to him. Stroking her cheek with the back of his hand, he said, "Do not let his words needle you, milady. I know why he hates me."

"As I do." She rose, knowing the danger of remaining so close to him. "He is jealous of the respect you receive from your men. Why don't you go to another thane who will appreciate your talents?"

"Do you want me to leave now that your future husband is here?" he asked as he stood.

Her fingers rested on his sleeves. "How can you ask me that?"

"Because if I had ever considered leaving, I would do so before I must watch you given to another man."

She shivered. Past the curtain, she could see the great hall where the ceremony would be performed. With no wedding feast, by this time tomorrow, she would be sharing her husband's bed.

Brenwyn's hands brought her back against his strong chest. She closed her eyes and lost herself in the sweetness of his touch.

"Do not leave me, Brenwyn," she whispered. "I need to know you are here when . . . only having you near will enable me to—"

"I will stay as long as I can, milady."

She whirled out of his arms to gaze up into his drawn face. "As long as you can? You are planning to leave!"

"Nothing is certain in these uneasy days. I will make no promises to you that I may not be able to keep. You know that."

"It is not right that I ask you to stay when another thane could give you the rank you deserve."

He smiled. "That was the most noble speech I have ever heard from one of your rank, milady."

Laughing, he put his hands on her elbows. He raised her hands to his lips. He kissed one, then the other. "Cyndra, I have told you I will stay with you as long as I can. That is a vow I swear with my life."

His hands slipped along her shoulders to her back and brought her against him. Combing her fingers through his thick hair, she steered his mouth over hers. His lips touched hers with sweet passion for a pair of heartbeats, then, without speaking, he released her and strode out of the stable.

Cyndra watched as he walked away. She must put him out of her life, but she had no idea how, for he had found a place in her heart.

Seven

Cyndra did not pretend to eat. She sat at the raised table with Morcar and Athelbert. Brenwyn had been consigned to a spot below the middle of the lower table. Morcar was determined to demean him. Did Morcar suspect her thoughts about Brenwyn? No, he must not guess, for, if he had, Brenwyn would be dead.

In silence, with a smile fixed on her face, she endured Morcar's bragging of things he could not have accomplished in a single lifetime. His listing of his wealth and powerful position in the king's favor did not impress her. Anyone could curry favor with Ethelred with a promise of gifts or higher taxes.

At meal's end, Morcar said, "Milady, I shall escort you to your bur."

Cyndra wished she could think of a reason to refuse. "I would be honored, Morcar."

She placed her hand over his, staring at the door. As he led her around the fire pit, she did not look at Brenwyn. His kiss had urged her to be strong, and she must be.

Morcar said nothing as they left the hall behind them. When they were only two steps past the pool of light that flowed from the doorway, he twisted

her into his arms and kissed her as he had upon
his arrival.

"Put your arms around me," he snarled. "Maidenly modesty is fine for a virgin, but you will be the
mother of my heirs."

"You are giving me no time to know you," she
protested. "I had thought you would—"

"You had thought I would woo you with gentle
caresses and longing looks." His hand settled on her
breast and his fingers pressed painfully into her. He
smiled at her soft cry of anguish. "You are mine.
Tomorrow, when we are wed and there can be no
question of the legitimacy of my heir, you will welcome me to your bed."

"Tomorrow, yes, but do not touch me tonight."
She shoved away his hands.

With a growl, he raised his fist. She stared in disbelief as it swung toward her. She leaped aside with
the instincts she had honed while helping Sigestan
learn to use his sword. He grabbed her full sleeve.
Threads ripped with a shriek, leaving her sleeve falling down her arm. His fingers dug into her arm as
he whirled her back toward him.

"Oh, milady, I thought I had sewed that sleeve
more securely," came Gleineth's voice. The maid
hurried forward, horror on her face. She dipped
into a quick curtsy, then said, "I assure you, milord,
I will not be so careless with milady's gown again."

He mumbled something as he released Cyndra's
arm. For a moment, she could not do anything but
stare. He was letting her go? Why had he come to
his senses?

As Gleineth put her arm around her, herding her
toward the bur as she kept up a loud babble of nonsense about the ripped sleeve and a whisper of how

Brenwyn had sent her to follow the thane and her lady, Cyndra looked back. In the door to the great hall stood a silhouette she could not mistake for any other.

She was not sure why Morcar had halted when Brenwyn appeared, but she could only be grateful that Brenwyn meant to keep his vow to protect her . . . no matter what.

In the glow before dawn, Cyndra rose. She had found no escape in sleep. Each time she closed her eyes, she saw Brenwyn's face as he turned to walk back into the great hall last night. She did not challenge her lurching stomach with breakfast.

Today, she must marry Morcar.

Gleineth said, "Milady, you should have something to eat."

"I swear by every saint that I shall sicken if I do."

"You will grow faint if you do not."

She laughed tersely. "Do you think Morcar would be offended if I fell senseless in the middle of our wedding ceremony or do you think he would even notice in his eagerness to have it completed?"

The maid dropped to the bench and hid her face in her hands. "If we could appeal to your father—"

"He would not halt this wedding. My father does not ignore his obligations. Neither do I."

"But this is wrong!"

Unable to argue with that, Cyndra did not reply. She paced the small chamber, then paused to close the doors on the bed. She would not be able to shut Morcar out of her life so easily . . . nor Brenwyn.

Gleineth rose stiffly when a knock sounded. Opening the door to reveal a lad, she asked, "Is it time?"

The boy shook his head. "Tell milady that the wedding ceremony cannot be held."

"Why?" Cyndra asked, pushing past her maid.

"There is no priest."

"I know the priest here is gone, but—"

"You do not understand, milady. All the priests within a day's ride have been called away by the bishop. None are expected back for weeks."

She put her hand up to her lips to hide her smile as she whispered, "Thank you for bringing me those tidings."

"My pleasure, milady." He bowed quickly and hurried away, his step jaunty as no one's had been since Morcar's return.

She did not close the door, but slipped out to look around the bailey. When she heard shouts from the far side, she saw Brenwyn training his men to use a spike to gain a foothold on a wall. He turned, and the distance between them melted as he smiled.

Behind her, Gleineth whispered, "I don't know how he did it, milady, but—"

"No one did anything!" She pulled her maid back into the bur. "No one must suggest that anyone did anything."

"I understand." The redhead grinned. "But I wonder how Brenwyn managed to convince the bishop to call a meeting of all the priests just now."

"I wonder as well." Her joy tempered as she went to the window and listened to the cheers from where the *fyrd* was working. No ceorl could manage such a feat. Who was Brenwyn of Manor Darburgh?

Cyndra smiled as she gave the servants today's tasks. This morning, Morcar had complained bitterly that no priests were at any burgh, even within a two-day ride. Only his determination to have no man question the legitimacy of his heir kept him from giving in to the lust in his eyes. She wondered how much longer he would wait to force her into his bed.

Hearing heavy footfalls, Cyndra looked up to see four unfamiliar men enter the hall. She locked the storeroom before she went to greet the strangers.

"Lady Cyndra?" asked one. He was gaunt, but strong muscles rippled beneath his short-sleeved tunic. Light brown hair, several shades darker than his near-white beard, dropped past his shoulders.

"Yes. How may I help you?" She hesitated, but could not halt her fear from blurting out with, "Are you holy men?"

"We are looking for Brenwyn, milady," he said with an odd accent. She wondered if he were from the Danelaw, where it was rumored that even the English spoke strangely. "We are not priests, but allies."

"I shall send a lad to find Brenwyn," she said calmly, even though all the ceorls must know how pleased she was that these men were not priests. "Is there a message you wish to send?"

"By your leave, milady, tell Brenwyn his friend Geoor is here."

Cyndra sent one of the boys cleaning a fire pit running to alert Brenwyn of Geoor's arrival. While she ordered food and drink brought, she kept her eyes lowered. Morcar would be furious that she treated a ceorl's friends with such generosity.

The men were finishing their mead when Brenwyn strode through the door. He hesitated for only a single pace as he looked at her. She wanted to thank him for what he must have done to halt the wedding. She could not.

With a smile, Brenwyn gripped Geoor's arm in greeting. Something pressed between his arm and chest. Quickly, he hid the rolled hides beneath his tunic.

"Thank you for being so gracious, milady," Brenwyn said. "If you will excuse us . . ."

"Brenwyn?"

He waited for Cyndra to continue, but she simply stared at him. His hand rose to cup her face. With a curse she could not understand, he turned and walked to the door. He paused and said, "Milady, I would, by your leave, speak to you later on a matter concerning your horse."

"I shall be here in the hall most of the day."

"I shall not be long."

She turned away, but not before he saw the flare of anticipation in her eyes. "When you can, Brenwyn."

"Yes, milady." Although he longed to put his arms around her and ease the pain of her heart, he motioned for his friend to follow him.

Brenwyn gave Geoor and his men a swift tour of the bailey. He pointed out how the manor was guarded so no one might sneak in without being observed. He compared the defenses of the manor with the others in the area. During his year at Manor Darburgh, he had visited neighboring burghs to learn how they protected themselves. The commanders of the other *fyrd*s had been proud to share their secrets with him, as he was now with his companions, who listened intently.

"What is it, Brenwyn?" queried Geoor as they walked past the back gate. "You do not seem yourself today." When Brenwyn did not answer, he chuckled. "It is a woman."

"Our problems are always women, aren't they?"

"Mayhap mine, but you have never neglected your duty." He chuckled. "She must be special."

"Very."

Geoor's eyes grew round. "Lady Cyndra?"

How had he betrayed himself? Of was it simply that Geoor knew him so well from the time they had served together?

"She is the thane's lady, Brenwyn!" Geoor grasped his arm. "Are you mad? You have worked years to get where you are now. Will you throw it away on someone else's betrothed? You must not cause trouble now."

"I know what I must do." Kneeling, he went on. "This is what *you* must do. Here is the route to your destination."

The men watched Brenwyn draw a map with a stick in the dirt. When they understood the directions, Brenwyn used his foot to erase the map back into the dust.

"How long?" Geoor asked.

"One fortnight, mayhap two. No longer."

"I thought you might know something more."

"Nothing."

"And if you did," the thin man said with a chuckle, "you would say nothing. You have earned your reputation for being closemouthed." With a farewell, he led the men out of the manor.

In the shadow of the wall, Brenwyn opened the packet Geoor had smuggled to him. Quickly, he read the information there. Geoor was correct. The situation was changing.

Another hide fell to the ground. Picking it up, he

frowned when he saw the order for him to come to the king's court immediately. He went into the nearest outbuilding and placed all but the hide with the orders from the king in the fire pit. He watched the other sheets turn brown and disintegrate, then looked again at the letter.

This was not going to be easy.

How much longer could things continue at this impasse? Cyndra sat at the raised table and glowered at her food. She had edged to the far right of her chair to put as much space between her and Morcar as possible. He had not spoken once to her since she entered the great hall this evening. Mayhap because he had heard the snickers about how he had been outsmarted by his betrothed and her serving maid.

When she heard Morcar agree sourly to have a ceorl approach the table, she stiffened as Brenwyn announced himself. Other than a quick bow of his head, he did not look in her direction. Why was he giving Morcar a chance to belittle him again before the whole burgh?

"Thane Morcar," Brenwyn said, "I have been commanded by the king to appear before him. I beg your leave to depart in the morning from Manor Darburgh."

"What nonsense is this? When has King Ethelred wished to see a worthless ceorl?"

Brenwyn's jaw tightened at the insult, but he handed a page to Morcar, who read it, then gave it to Athelbert. When Cyndra tried to see what was written on the hide, Athelbert turned away to block her view.

Laughing, Athelbert sneered, "King Ethelred wants to see *you*, Brenwyn? He recognizes a kindred fool."

Cyndra lowered her eyes. Brenwyn was leaving? Mayhap he would take her with him. When she glanced at him, he shook his head slightly in answer to her unvoiced question. Horror clamped around her.

Morcar grabbed the page and flung it at Brenwyn's feet. Going to the wall, he took down a shield that she knew was Brenwyn's. He threw it to the floor and broke it under his foot.

Cyndra gasped as the room became utterly silent. By breaking the shield, he was releasing Brenwyn from his oath to Manor Darburgh and to Morcar.

"Go," snarled Morcar, "and call upon our king who has proven his stupidity. Leave Manor Darburgh, and do not return."

She was not the only one to choke back astonishment at Brenwyn's banishment. *No!* When Morcar scowled at her, she feared she had said that aloud.

Picking up the letter, Brenwyn nodded. "It shall be as you request, milord. I will leave with the coming of the sun, and I will serve you no more." His voice was strangely calm for a man stripped of his position. "I bid you farewell, milord, milady."

He spun on his heel and retrieved his spear from the stack by the door. Without a backward glance, he was gone.

A hand on Cyndra's shoulder tried to convey Gleineth's sympathy. Cyndra did not move. She must be careful.

Morcar turned to her. "What, milady? Do I see sadness on your face? You mourn the loss of a ceorl?"

"Brenwyn took such good care of my steed, milord," she answered calmly.

"Your steed? Is that all he tended for you?" His bony fingers dug into her wrist.

"Milord, he is only a ceorl. What are you intimating?"

"Let no other man play a part in your life but your betrothed."

Her eyebrows raised with her wrath. "Such a warning is unnecessary and insulting."

Patting her face, he turned to Athelbert. Through the long meal, Cyndra said nothing more. She listened to the talk around her and watched the dancers perform to the minstrels' music. Wild applause greeted the female dancers who slithered sensuously across the floor.

"Morcar, may I have your permission to retire?" she asked when she heard cheers from Athelbert as a dancer reached to loosen her tunic.

"Begone, and take your dreary face with you."

Rising, she led Gleineth out the back door. In her bur, she sank onto the bench by the fire.

"Go with him," urged Gleineth.

"Go . . . with him?" she repeated in shock. "You want me to go with Brenwyn?"

"Aye, milady. Go with Brenwyn." She knelt and whispered, "He goes to the king, milady. Let him take you there. Once you find powerful allies, you need not return here."

Cyndra wanted to laugh at her maid's innocence. "How would I obtain these allies?"

"Your jewelry?"

"It would not buy too many ears, for they cost highly." Standing, she leaned her hands on the door to the bed.

"But you must go with Brenwyn! He will help you."

Cyndra shook her head. "I cannot. Morcar will be watching. He suspects I feel more for Brenwyn than is proper. Brenwyn has been banished from Manor Darburgh and I will be kept here, so our paths will never cross again."

"But, milady, if—"

"No!" cried Cyndra. "I will not endanger his life! I wish to hear no more of this. Never again, Gleineth. Do you understand?"

Meekly, she replied, "Yes, Lady Cyndra, I understand."

Cyndra sat as Gleineth went to her own bed. Music sifted across the bailey to her until she shut the room's single window. She must go to bed, too, because she did not want to sleep past dawn and miss seeing Brenwyn one last time.

Sitting in her lightweight underdress, she braided her hair before she climbed into her bed. Gleineth's snores were a soft undercurrent to the night insects' songs, but she could not sleep as she stared at the roof.

A soft knock startled the night silence.

Throwing a tunic over her shoulders, Cyndra reached for the latch. "Brenwyn!" She pulled him into the bur and closed the door. "Why are you here at this hour?"

He put out his hand to caress her hair. With a gentle smile, he asked, "Did you think I would leave without saying farewell, milady?"

"It is kind of you. I appreciate the service you have given to me and—"

"Enough, Cyndra!"

He gripped her shoulders and lowered his mouth

over hers. His arms swept around her and pulled her to his strong body.

Frightened of being discovered in his arms, she froze for a moment. Then her yearning dissolved her into honeyed sweetness against him. For this pleasure, she would risk all. Her arms arched along his back as he explored the moist secrets of her mouth. The stroke of his tongue on hers fired her desire. She was swirled away into a tempest far more powerful than any summer storm. As he bent her back against his arm, she explored the firm lines of his body that enticed her fingers.

When he whispered for her to open her eyes, she obeyed slowly. She did not want to leave this dream. Her hand rose to comb through his hair and guide his mouth back to hers. For this one moment, she could give in to her fantasies.

"No," he urged. "Listen to me."

"I would rather you use your mouth to kiss me."

"As I would." He kissed her lightly. "I must go."

"Go now? What is wrong?"

"When I hold you, nothing should be wrong, but I suspect Morcar hopes to arrange my death beyond these walls at dawn." Pulling a knife from his belt, he pressed its haft into her palm. "I hope you will not need this."

She balanced the blade in her hand. "I pray that you are right, but I am not afraid to fight."

"I know." He caught her by the shoulders. "Stay strong, and I will return for you."

"Return? You are banished from Manor Darburgh forever."

His eyes twinkled. "I will return for you, milady. That is a vow I make to you, and I have told you more than once that I only make vows that I intend to keep."

"Do not be foolish."

"I am not. That is why I must go, milady, while I can." He drew her lips under his for a final kiss. "Farewell until I return, my sweet lady."

He was gone before Cyndra could move. She stared at the closed door. Her fingers remained outstretched, but they held only emptiness.

Eight

The burgh grew bleak. The days were tolerable, but in the evening, decent behavior disappeared from the hall. Several ceorls approached Cyndra to request that their women be excused from attending the evening meals. She hesitated, not wanting to enrage Morcar further. The thane was furious that Brenwyn had evaded his deadly trap.

Morcar turned Brenwyn's duties as commander of the *fyrd* over to Athelbert. The thane accepted the title and ignored the *fyrd*. The men grew restive, but Cyndra had no inkling of the depth of the trouble until Cerdic sought her out a week after Brenwyn had left.

"I must speak with you, milady," he whispered. "Not here in the hall."

Cyndra's heart trembled as she recalled Brenwyn saying similar words. Now he was gone. The tears she refused to let fall thickened in her throat, so she nodded, afraid to trust her voice.

She walked out of the hall with him. Cerdic should have been named Brenwyn's successor. Although Cerdic had said nothing, she had heard that Morcar's hatred was now aimed at him.

"Mayhap," she said, "I should not be seen speaking with you." She scanned the bailey.

"Thane Morcar is beyond the walls, hunting."

She nodded again, glad that he understood what she did not dare to say aloud.

His voice remained close to a whisper. "There is not a man here who is unaware of the peril. Not after last night."

"What happened?" she asked as they stopped by the kitchen.

"It is not pretty telling."

"I am a warrior's daughter."

A smile flashed across his taut lips. "You will need every skill you inherited from your father. Once the Norse raiders were our greatest enemy. Now I fear our thane will destroy us before the Vikings can."

"What do you mean?"

He squared his shoulders. "Milady, I know Ecgbert and others have approached you to ask permission to keep their women from the hall. I beseech you to reconsider. Last night, after you and Gleineth retired, Athelbert decided he wanted a ceorl's woman. The ceorl, Higbald, was slain, and Athelbert took Higbald's woman to his bur. She was found dead this morning."

"No one halted Athelbert?" she asked past her horror.

"We tried." He pointed to his left sleeve, and she noticed, for the first time, that his arm was thick with bandages.

"Tell the ceorls to keep their women from the hall. I cannot give the men the same permission."

"For whatever you can do, we are grateful."

"How does the *fyrd* do?"

"We do nothing! Athelbert refuses to allow me to

train the men, for he fears that Morcar will see he is useless. So we sit and wait for them to prey upon us."

Hesitating, she lowered her voice. "By all the saints, leave as Brenwyn did."

"I have sworn my life to protect this burgh. Such a vow I hold until death."

Cyndra understood too well, for she was constrained by vows she wished had never been made. As Cerdic rushed away as the gates opened for Morcar and his hunting party, she wondered how long it would be before all their vows ended with death.

Cyndra woke to screams. She sat up and stared into the darkness. What was Morcar doing now to torture the people of Manor Darburgh?

She flinched when she heard another shriek. It could not be Morcar. He had left with the *fyrd* days ago, called away by the king to fight the Norse attack along England's shores. She jumped out of bed.

"Milady, milady!" Gleineth groped out of the darkness to grasp her shoulder. "We are lost!"

"Lost? What is happening out there?" She reached for the door.

Her maid caught her hands. "No, milady. You cannot go out there. I peeked through the window. We are lost!"

"Why? What is—?"

"Jomsvikings! I saw them. Jomsvikings here in Manor Darburgh!"

Cyndra sighed and tried to force the fear out of her. "The Jomsvikings are fighting for our king." The Norse mercenaries sold their services to the highest bidder. She pushed past Gleineth. "If give them shelter and food, they will leave us in peace."

A furtive knock sounded on the door. She opened it before Gleineth could halt her.

A ceorl knelt and seized Cyndra's hand. "Milady, help us!"

"Give the Jomsvikings what food they wish. Then they will leave."

"They want Manor Darburgh," he cried.

"You must be mistaken."

He shook his head so hard she feared it would fly off. "Milady, they burst through the gate. They are demanding that Manor Darburgh surrender."

Cyndra did not hesitate. These Jomsvikings must be renegades. "Tell everyone to flee. We are not a *fyrd*. Go!"

"Milady, you must—"

"Go to Manor Tiwburgh," she ordered, although the burgh was a day's walk during the daylight. At night, she could not guess how long it would take. "Go while you can!"

He vanished into the darkness.

Cyndra closed the door. Grasping her tunic, she flung it around her shoulders. It would be too dangerous to light a lamp. They had to sneak out of the bur and out of the manor.

"Milady, what are we going to do?"

"We are going to Manor Tiwburgh. Follow me." She grabbed her small box of jewelry and shoved it into Gleineth's hands.

She reached under her pillow where she kept Brenwyn's knife while she slept. Her fingers trembled as she slipped it in the sash of her tunic. She did not want to use it; but, as she had proven with the Vikings near Manor Saeburgh, she would not hesitate if attacked.

Manor Saeburgh . . . if the Vikings were here, what had happened there? Father had sent her here to be safe from the Vikings. Now . . . she choked back a gasp. By all the saints, had Manor Saeburgh fallen?

She must think only of escaping now. She opened the door and heard screams and sounds of fighting. Light shone from the great hall. In the glow, she could see many forms moving without fear. This was more than a foray. This was a full invasion.

They had to escape!

Before Cyndra could move, a shadow blocked the door. She swallowed her scream. Gleineth shrieked behind her.

She groped for her knife. The Jomsviking laughed as he blocked her motion with his broadsword.

Gleineth screamed again, more desperately.

Cyndra tried to inch her hand past his weapon. With another laugh, he slapped her fingers away with the flat of his blade. She gasped in astonishment. She had not expected such a Viking to be playful. Or was his taunting only a prelude to torture? She took a deep breath. She would not give him the satisfaction of begging to be spared.

He grasped her arm and pulled her out of the bur. When another man stepped before the door to guard it, he herded her across the wet grass, ignoring Gleineth's cries to spare her lady.

He shoved her through the door of the hall. Among the mailed warriors, she could see a few of her ceorls cowering in the corners. Hope filled her. Mayhap the others had escaped to safety.

She was forced to her knees. Angrily, she rose. She

was the daughter of an ealdorman. She would not kneel to the Viking scourge.

The warrior snarled. She pulled her knife. Before she could slash it at him, he struck her viciously. She collapsed, every bone jarred.

A shout silenced the room. Raising her head, she saw leather shoes and cross-gartered stockings coming toward her. The warrior answered in an awed tone, and she knew he was speaking to his commander. She silently cursed both of them to endure every torture in hell.

Cyndra struggled to her knees. Her head reeled with pain, but she must plead for clemency for her people. Her pride meant nothing in comparison with their lives.

"I beg you," she said with all the dignity she could find. "Do not hurt the ceorls here. I offer you my keys to the storerooms, if you spare my household." Picking up the knife, she raised it over her head in both hands like a liege vowing his oath of allegiance.

A finger in a thick, leather glove tilted her chin. "No one who cooperates will be hurt, especially not you, Cyndra."

She gasped at the familiar voice. Her gaze rose along the warrior's mail to the blue-green eyes she knew so well. Although his black hair was covered by the engraved, conical helmet that narrowed to a nosepiece in the center of his face, she recognized him with the ease of the joy in her pounding heart.

"Brenwyn!" Shock silenced her. Why was Brenwyn dressed like a Jomsviking?

"I do not like seeing you kneel to me, milady."

He brought her to her feet. He pulled off his helmet. With his arm around her waist, he captured her mouth. As she softened against his hard body, she could not silence the questions careening through her head. Brenwyn should not be dressed like this! There must be an explanation.

He smiled. "Do not be afraid, milady."

"Brenwyn—"

"Say no more now."

Cyndra nodded, knowing her curiosity could destroy them both.

"Milady, go with Harald to your bur. I will send for you later to explain why you are now a prisoner."

"Explain? You said you were going to serve the king!"

His smile froze her blood in her veins. "I am serving my king, milady. My king is Swein Forkbeard." His fingers reached out to caress her cheek, but she jerked away.

"Don't!" All her life, she had hated the Vikings. She did not want to love one. Love? Dear God, she had loved Ceorl Brenwyn. She could not love this Jomsviking he had become, betraying her with a web of lies.

His eyes darkened with rage. "Cyndra, think well on your situation."

"If you expect me to be a traitor, too, you are mistaken. My king is Ethelred."

"Soon England shall bow before her new master." He tugged her against him and smiled coldly. "England shall be conquered more easily than you."

Cyndra stared at him. She had fallen in love with a man who did not exist. The tender Brenwyn whose touch had thrilled her was not this Viking. Her eyes filled with tears as the vision of him in his mail blurred to become the Brenwyn who had comforted her after she had met Morcar.

Morcar!

"Brenwyn," she whispered, "have you killed Morcar?"

"He may be dead, milady, but not at my hand. Go to your bur. You will understand later."

Cyndra did not protest when a Jomsviking took her to where a man with a bared sword stood outside her bur. He stepped aside. She was shoved inside, and the door slammed shut. Arms were flung around her, and she heard hysterical sobbing.

"I am unhurt, Gleineth. I was taken to meet their commander. They hold Manor Darburgh now."

Gleineth sat on the bench. "Where is Morcar and the *fyrd*, milady?"

"Morcar, if he is alive, is far from here. Bren—"

"Brenwyn also is miles away."

"Brenwyn is here." Leaning her head on her arms atop the windowsill, she whispered, "He is here. He is the leader of this raiding party."

"Brenwyn?"

"He has betrayed us to our enemies." With a terse laugh, she said, "He *is* our enemy."

In a quivering voice, Gleineth asked, "What are you going to do, milady?"

"He is a Jomsviking, Gleineth. What choice do I have? I must submit to his wishes or I shall die."

"Brenwyn cares for you."

"Does he? Or was that another lie?" Before Gleineth could answer, she went on, "We must sleep while we can. If a chance comes to escape, we must be ready."

"Do you think it will?"

"No. We will be watched too closely."

"Because he doesn't want to lose you again, milady."

When Cyndra did not answer, Gleineth went to her cot.

Cyndra blew out the lamp and got into bed. She did not remove her tunic. Staring at the roof of her bed, she tried to accept the truth. In his position as leader of the *fyrd* of Manor Darburgh, Brenwyn had been privy to the weaknesses of the nearby burghs. Had those manors been overrun tonight, too?

When Brenwyn kissed her tonight, her delight at his eager touch was the only thing unchanged. She had been betrayed by her longing for his love.

No tears burned in her eyes as she slipped into a sleep that was dreamless. She had no fear of nightmares. All of them had come true while she was awake.

Nine

When the door opened at dawn, Cyndra looked up, expecting to see the guard. Her gaze was caught by Brenwyn's. She rose and faced him, wondering if he had slept more than she had last night.

"May I come in, milady?" Brenwyn asked, as if nothing had changed. She almost could believe that, because he wore his customary clothes.

"Do I have any choice?"

His mouth tightened. "You have very few alternatives at this point."

"Then I must invite you into my bur, Brenwyn. Please sit." She stepped back. "Is your name still Brenwyn or some unpronounceable Norse name?"

He gripped her arms. "Cyndra, don't be stupid. Others will not be as accepting of your insults as I am."

"I will never bow my head to a traitor and his Viking king." Knowing it was futile, she battled his strength.

His fingers pushed back her veil to sift through her hair. "I am Brenwyn as I was before, although my full name is Brenwyn Gunnarsson."

"Gunnarsson?" she whispered, relenting in her

struggle. The name oddly seemed to make this more real than anything else.

"My name does not matter. What matters is that I want you as mine. That has not changed."

"Too much else has!" Trying to believe her own lies, she asserted, "I do not want anything to do with you. How many burghs did you destroy last night? How many have suffered?"

Brenwyn smiled. Cyndra was undaunted by her captivity. She remained the proud beauty who had tempted him to put aside his mission so he could win her heart.

He slipped his arm around her and pulled her gentle curves to him as he found her mouth. When her soft breath grew unsteady, her hands encircled his shoulders. He pressed his lips to her throat, tasting her sweet skin. Greedily, he recaptured her mouth.

He gazed at her. She was lovely in her soft robes. As her fingers stroked his face, he tipped his head to kiss her palm. He brushed her hair back and knew he did not need to explain that he had delayed taking her with him because he had known that soon he would return for her.

He looked at the bed. The raid would have been perfect if her sniveling betrothed had met his end here. But that was no longer important. Morcar was gone, hopefully dead. Cyndra was here and in his arms.

"You and Gleineth will be unharmed, milady," he said, "but you must stay in your bur."

"Why?"

"Because that is my order."

"Brenwyn, I—"

"You will, Cyndra," he said sharply. When he saw

the pain on her face, he walked to the door. "I will escort you to the evening meal."

"With your Jomsvikings?" She shook her head. "I shall not break bread with my enemies."

"That was also an order, milady." He ran his fingers along her cheek. "Wear your best robes tonight to honor our victory. The Jomsvikings fight for their king once more and have secured this valley. You will see much coming and going today. My men will be arriving to give their reports."

"Your men? You are in charge of this whole foray?"

He chuckled at her astonishment. "The rôle of a ceorl was not easy for a man who holds a rank equal to that of an ealdorman. You told me more than once you could not understand why I did not obtain land to become a thane. Now, mayhap, you will begin to understand."

He left her staring after him. She was beginning to understand . . . how little she understood about this man who had touched her heart.

When twilight crept across the burgh, Cyndra rose from the bench by the window to dress for the evening meal. She had spent the day trying to sort out her confusion as she watched the ceorls go about their tasks. They were the same, although Jomsvikings walked the wall and more poured through the gate to bring news to Brenwyn.

She let Gleineth help her pull on her finest underdress and a tunic of saffron wool. On her girdle of decorated linen were attached the six-inch-long girdle hangers of silver. She had received them on her twelfth birthday, for they symbolized the key ring no housewife would be without. On her left arm, she wore a wide, golden arm-ring decorated with amethysts. When her veil was placed over her neatly coiffed hair, she affixed it in place with strands of gold and pearls.

Cyndra looked in the burnished shield on the wall to see her blurred reflection. All that was missing was the smile which would have accented her glittering jewels. That she could not find. Her hypocrisy taunted her.

She was latching on her favorite pendant when a knock sounded.

Gleineth rushed to the door and dropped into a curtsy to Brenwyn. "Good evening . . . milord."

"Good evening, Gleineth." He gave her a smile before his gaze met Cyndra's. It slipped along her in a slow appraisal that left embers of desire in its wake.

No, she did not want to be caught up in the game of passion that was entangled with this war. She longed to return to the simpler days when her only worries had been making sure there was food and lodging for her father's guests.

"Your servant, milord." Her voice trembled as she dipped into a deep curtsy.

He took her fingers and raised her to her feet. Lifting her hand to his lips, he kissed it gently. "Milady, I told you before I did not want you kneeling to me."

"I do not know how to act with a man who was once a ceorl and now is my captor."

"Not your captor, milady." His finger traced her cheekbone, and his voice grew husky. "If you wish to return to Morcar, I shall have you sent to him."

She gazed up into his eyes. He was serious. Brenwyn had not changed. A surge of hope filled her heart. "I do not wish to go back to him."

"You would rather stay with me?"

She laughed, startling herself. "I cannot say *yes,* for I am very confused."

"About me?"

"Yes."

He kissed her cheek. "Do not be."

"Brenwyn, are my father and brother alive?" She could not hold back the question.

"I do not know." He sighed. "I know only of what has happened here. I shall not know more until I receive word from my leader, Thevkil the Strong."

She shivered at the name she knew too well from the tales of butchery throughout England. "Thevkil is your leader?"

Instead of answering, he held out his hand. "Milady?"

She placed her hand on top of his. He said nothing as they walked toward the hall. Glancing at him from beneath her lowered lashes, she saw the taut line of his lips. What was he not telling her? She was not sure she wished to know.

Cyndra kept her head high as she entered the hall. Black banners draped from the rafters. Shields hung on the walls. Each was embossed with a thunderbolt or a raven. Beneath them were stacked battle-axes. It was as if she had been transported to Jylland.

The Jomsvikings stood. They bowed their heads toward Brenwyn, but every eye was on her. When she heard a snicker, she tensed, but Brenwyn did not slow as he led her to the raised table.

He introduced her to his men sitting there. Each bowed and acted as if they did not notice her unease with her enemies. She maintained her calm until Brenwyn brought her to meet his second-in-command.

"Geoor!" she gasped as the gaunt man bowed his head to her. "You came here to see Brenwyn." She was shocked anew at their daring.

He laughed. "It is an honor to meet you again, Lady Cyndra. As ever, you are an excellent hostess."

"I am not your hostess. This burgh is no longer mine."

"That, I am sure, is only a temporary situation, my lady. I am—"

"That is enough, Geoor," Brenwyn said. "Do not discuss publicly what Lady Cyndra and I have not had an opportunity to discuss privately."

Cyndra glanced at him, but his smile told her nothing. Did Brenwyn intend to remain here?

Brenwyn refused to allow her to serve the men at the raised table, insisting that she was their guest. As she listened to their rollicking voices, she wondered if these could be the same demons who had haunted her childhood sleep.

She quickly discovered that Brenwyn planned to teach her what she must know to fit into his Norse world. As he handed her a cup or plate, he spoke its name in the Norse tongue and told her to repeat it.

"If you expect me to learn that language," she said, "I must warn you it is a hopeless task."

"You will learn, milady. Our two languages are not so different." He held his goblet to her lips. "Drink, milady."

When she had taken a sip, he tilted the cup to his mouth. He drank, then held it out to her. She leaned forward to drink from it, but gasped as his arm pressed her to him. He kissed her deeply. When she heard cheers, she stiffened.

No matter what Brenwyn might say, his men saw her as a prize he had won. He had conquered Thane Morcar's manor. Now he was proving his mastery over the thane's lady. A hot wave of shame flashed through her.

Brenwyn frowned. "Do you dislike my kisses?"

"I like your kisses too much for a woman betrothed to another man."

His blue eyes riveted her with hunger. "That is no more."

"You cannot change—"

"The contract is no more, for Thane Morcar of Manor Darburgh no longer exists. If he still lives, he is a landless outlaw in the land of his enemies." His hand curved along her cheek. "Cyndra, come with me."

She dared not defy his order. Although Brenwyn was not cruel like Morcar, she must never shame this proud man. She placed her hand in his.

As he led her from the high table, he shouted for another cask of ale to be tapped. The men bellowed their appreciation.

Cyndra took a deep breath of the warm air as they left the hall. Her whole world had been turned inside out. In silence, they walked to her bur.

Brenwyn paused at the door. When he drew her into his arms, he kissed her with eagerness. She fought not to respond, but it was impossible. She could no longer resist his touch.

"No more skulking in the shadows for us, milady," he whispered. "Now you are mine as I have longed from the moment I saw your lovely face by the stream."

"Morcar will learn of your attack upon Manor Darburgh and come back with his *fyrd*."

His laugh chilled her. "I hope he returns. I shall be waiting for him. For what he did to you, I would gladly see him dead at my feet." His gentle fingers stroking her face did not match his cold words. "Come, milady."

"But this is impossible. If—"

"It is an old saying among the Norse that no one can speak with surety what is possible when two hearts call out to each other." He opened the door and motioned for her to enter. Her eyes widened as she saw her bur was lit with a wealth of candles.

He smiled as he brought her into his arms. "I could endure waiting no longer," he murmured as he laced his fingers through her hair. "I have waited so long for you. Now you will be mine."

She was given no chance to reply, for he captured her mouth. He kissed her with an eagerness that demanded she give up the pretense that she did not want him. Her desires spun through her as his fingers discovered sensations along her that she had not guessed existed.

"Brenwyn—"

"Hush, milady. Listen to your heart answering mine. Then you will know the truth." He lifted the drape of her veil and pushed aside her hair to kiss the rapid pulse in her neck. Despite herself, she shivered in anticipation.

He teased her ear with his tongue. Her hands gripped his arms as her knees threatened to buckle beneath the sweet assault. When his fingers touched the sensitive skin of her breast, she moaned softly.

He pulled the ring from his cloak to let the material drift to the floor, and his throaty laugh sent fire racing through her. When he undid her gown to let it fall at her feet, he ran a single finger between her breasts. She could not silence her moan or the need to touch him. Raising trembling fingers, she brought his mouth to hers.

He leaned her back on her bed, and she reveled in the exquisite sensations within her. Nothing ever had been like this. Even their stolen kisses had been such a weak prelude to this pleasure. Through her thin robe, his fingers seared her breasts.

He pulled off his sword belt and dropped it to the floor. Sitting on the edge of the bed, he ran his fingers along her bare arm. When he lifted her fingers to the brooch at his shoulder, she plucked it out to loosen his clothes. Her gaze was held by his when he guided her fingers to the sash at his waist. Her efforts to release its knot were hampered by his kisses along her shoulders. When the sash was undone, he shrugged aside his tunic.

She gazed at him in wonder. His strong muscles urged her fingers to caress them. She knelt. While he slid her underdress along her, she pressed her naked body to his. Another soft moan escaped her lips. His skin was so warm, and each touch incited her to a flame.

She was so bemused by the flurry of kisses across her face, she barely noticed him tossing aside her underdress. His groan of desire awakened needs she had never known. She drew him down onto the bed with her. When his tongue caressed her breast, she could not still the motion of her eager body.

She murmured his name as his fingers grazed her thigh, but she could think only of the lightning-hot tingles across her skin. Her fingers glided past his heartbeat and along his chest. Growing more bold in her need, she followed his strong muscles to his hips. The varied textures of his body enticed her.

Caught in a fire storm, she opened her eyes to look up at him as he raised himself over her. His face mirrored her overpowering passions. He brought them together, banishing all thought. She steered his mouth over hers. At the touch of his lips, she ceded herself to a rapture that melded them into one ecstasy.

Brenwyn smiled when Cyndra's breath heated his bare chest. When he brushed back her hair, she opened her eyes a slit and caressed his cheek.

"Cyndra," he whispered, "this was even more wondrous than I dreamt."

She murmured something, then closed her eyes. She curled her body to fit perfectly against his side as he ran his hand along her golden hair. Almost everything he wanted was his. He could have chosen any burgh for his target. Instead of the richer Manor Tiwburgh, he had chosen Morcar's measly manor. It offered a single treasure, but he had vowed that no one else would have Cyndra.

Manor Darburgh was his. As he looked down at her head lying on his shoulder, he wondered if Cyndra would be as well. How many times had he told her in the past day that he had not changed? Neither had she. She might delight in his touch and share her delicious body with him, but her heart belonged to her England.

As his did, but to a different England. He wondered if what he wanted for them was possible.

"You're asking the impossible." Geoor's voice rang through his head.

"It is my order." His own voice had been even as they sat by the fire in the forest a day's ride from here.

In disgust, Geoor stated, "That order is ridiculous. How do we explain to our men that you wish to break the long-standing tradition that all of the possessions of the loser, including his women, belonged to the victor? You want us to grant the thane's lady her freedom? No one ever gave such an order."

"I have said this will be so, Geoor Scyldsson. You and your men may have any of the other women, but the thane's lady must be granted her freedom, if she wishes it."

Comprehension glowed in his second-in-command's eyes. "I understand, Brenwyn. You do not want the men to see your clemency for Morcar's lady as weakness." He sighed. "It will be a great sacrifice you ask us to make. Few of the other English women will be willing to become a thrall-concubine, as Lady Cyndra will for you."

His fist struck his shield. "She shall not be my thrall. She is the lady of Manor Darburgh, and she will be granted her freedom. If she wishes to return to Morcar, then that is how it shall be."

"By Thor's hammer, you love her!" Geoor made it sound like the worse curse to befall any man. "You fool! Keep her as your mistress, but do no more. It could cost you your rank. It could cost you your life! If she were any other woman, they would agree. To marry this one could be your death knell, Brenwyn."

"That is how it will have to be."

"Mayhap, but are you so sure she will choose you over returning to the English?"

He had wanted to say he was certain of that, but

he had not been. Not then, not now. He had to know.

Gently, he rolled her over onto her back and brushed her lips with his. As his body reacted to the warmth of her lips, he whispered her name. He had to know.

Her eyes opened, their sleepiness vanishing into a soft glow of happiness. Just as they had when she stood by her father the day Brenwyn came to Manor Saeburgh and she had been certain of what her future held. All of that had vanished, leaving only this pleasure to ward off the war around them.

"Cyndra," he whispered, "I know you want to know my plans for you and this burgh."

She blinked, and the softness vanished. "I can't be accused of letting you seduce secrets from me when you know this burgh better than I do."

"The only reason I seduced you is the only reason that matters. I want you to be my wife."

"You cannot be serious!"

"I have never been more serious, Cyndra."

"But I can't marry a . . ." She looked away.

"A Jomsviking? You will marry me, Cyndra. You will marry me and renounce your old ways."

"I can't! You ask too much of me."

"You will." His finger teased the tip of her breast. When she moaned and tried to push his hand away, he kissed her with all his yearning for her. She melted against him as he whispered, "As my wife, you will be mistress of a domain far larger than this small burgh. You will dress in fine garments. I have won jewels which wait for your beauty."

Her voice was soft with yearning. "Wealth is not worth betraying everything I hold dear."

"Marry me, and you will enjoy this treasure beyond price." His mouth claimed hers. He stroked her until she writhed. "Be mine now, Cyndra."

"I am yours now."

He knew he should not surrender to the passion twisting about them in a dance of delight, but he had become its captive as surely as she was. Dawn would be time enough to show her she must be his wife. For now . . . He groaned as her fingers slipped along him.

"Brenwyn, please, love me now."

With a grin, he answered, "It will be *our* pleasure, milady."

Ten

Brenwyn was gone when Cyndra awoke. For a horrifying moment, she feared her memories of passion were a dream. But then, Morcar would again be the nightmare that stalked her during day and night.

No, she was free of his cruelty . . . and the captive of her longing for Brenwyn.

Closing her eyes, she burrowed back into the bed as she recalled the joys she had discovered last night. She tried to recreate the delicious sensations from her memories. With a chuckle, she told herself not to worry. It would not be long before Brenwyn returned to her. He had been, she knew, as thrilled as she was with the delight they could offer each other.

The door opened, and she sat, pulling the covers to her chin. She smiled as Gleineth greeted her.

"Good morning, milady." There was a questioning tone to her words.

"It is a lovely morning, isn't it, Gleineth?"

The redhead smiled. "I am glad you think so."

"Do you?"

She bent to gather up Cyndra's clothes which had been tossed to the floor. "It is not as I thought it would be, milady, but it is good."

Cyndra wanted to hug her maid for understanding what she could not say. Both of them recalled how Gleineth had urged her to run away with Brenwyn. Now he had come back to Manor Darburgh to give Cyndra's fantasies life, although neither of them could have imagined he would claim the title of leader of this group of Jomsvikings.

When the maid handed her a clean tunic, Cyndra slipped it on. Her fingers ran through her hair, and she moaned when she encountered tangles from the night. She could not keep from smiling as she picked up her brush and began to attack the strands. Brenwyn's fingers had woven her hair together when they had slipped through it.

"Here, milady. Let me help you." Gleineth took the brush. "He requests that you join him for the morning meal."

"He wants me to marry him."

Gleineth sighed. "If only it were possible."

"He is determined it will be possible. I am to renounce all I was to become his wife. He intends to have a Norse wedding ceremony here as soon as everything can be arranged."

She paused in midstroke. "And you said, milady?"

"I said *yes*." She twisted on the bench as she heard Gleineth's gasp of horror. Putting her hand on Gleineth's arm, she looked at her maid with supplication. "I do not know what is right or wrong anymore. Everything I have always believed means I should be with Morcar, but Brenwyn makes me happy."

"It will break your father's heart, milady." Her eyes widened. "Forgive me for saying that."

Cyndra stood, her face icy. She wanted to believe Father and Sigestan were still alive; but if the Vikings were here, Manor Saeburgh must have fallen. "What you said was the truth."

"He will understand that you have no choice."

"But I do. Brenwyn gave me the choice of going back to Morcar, if I wish." Her voice grew granite hard. "I never want to see him again."

"How he loves you, milady!" Gleineth's face brightened. "I did not think even Brenwyn was brave enough to offer you a chance to go back to Morcar when you might have accepted just to escape the Vikings."

She twisted her hair onto her head and pinned it into place. "Even if I did not feel as I do for Brenwyn, I would not have gone to seek refuge with Morcar."

"You hate him that much?"

"Yes, I hate him that much." She smoothed her gown, thinking of Brenwyn's fingers gliding along her. How she wished he were here, driving all her trepidation from her with his fevered kisses! In his arms, she could not think of anything but rapture.

She turned to peer into the polished shield on the wall. She wanted to look her best for her future husband. Her heart leaped in response to that thought.

"He will be pleased with you," Gleineth said softly, "for his thoughts have been of no one but you from the moment he arrived at Manor Saeburgh." A hint of a sad smile curled along her lips. "You may trust that is so, milady, for when I tried to flirt with him, his words were only of you."

Cyndra whirled. "You flirted with Brenwyn?"

"I feared a dalliance with a ceorl would break your heart, milady. I thought he might be persuaded to consider one of his rank." She dropped to her knees. "If you wish to send me away—"

"Of course not." Putting her hands on Gleineth's shoulders, she smiled. "Brenwyn is a handsome man, and I know you like handsome men. That you wished to protect me as well is something I shall never forget." She motioned for her maid to come to her feet. "But do you want to leave?"

"Leave you here alone with these—" She flushed. "I will stay with you, if I may. You will need some help to civilize these Vikings." Her eyes twinkled as she glanced out the window. "And they are a handsome lot."

"I had thought you would notice." For the first time since they had left Manor Saeburgh, the sense of camaraderie that she had shared with her maid had returned. Only now did she realize how much her fear of Morcar had stolen from her.

"Go, Lady Cyndra. Brenwyn awaits you in the hall. You do not want to keep him waiting."

That Cyndra could agree with wholeheartedly. The sunshine was bright as she emerged from the bur. She tilted her face to enjoy the heat burning away the darkness left by Morcar. Although she had known infinite bliss in the past day, the bur had been a prison. Once more she was free.

She was not surprised to see the guard was gone from her door. Brenwyn need not worry about his loyal men any longer. He had made it clear she was his.

From what she could see, it looked like a normal day in the burgh. A greeting was called to her from the kitchen. Ceorls worked near the stables. Brenwyn had the loyalty of the ceorls here. Their hatred for Morcar made it easier for them to take an oath of fealty to Brenwyn Gunnarsson.

Cyndra walked past the open gate and paused to stare out past two guards who stood there, their axes bare in their thick hands.

The guards spoke in their Norse language and laughed as the taller one stepped in front of her. "You may not leave the burgh," he said with a thick accent. "That is the order of Brenwyn Gunnarsson."

She did not bother to argue. It was useless to say that she had not intended to leave. These men would not believe her.

Looking past them, she saw that the normally deserted road was a steady stream of people. The refugees carried their possessions on their backs. One family had an old dray they pulled behind them. They were broken people. No sounds of singing or conversation came from the slowly moving crowd. Even the children were subdued beneath their heavy loads.

It did no good to tell herself Brenwyn was different from the others. He was not. It was simply that she saw him as a man she loved first and a warrior second.

Hands on her shoulders did not have to be identified. Both the flush of warmth that filled her and the hatred on the refugees' faces told her Brenwyn stood behind her. The English scurried away before he noticed them.

Brenwyn ordered his men to resume their posts. He tugged on Cyndra's arm and drew her away from the palisade. As his arm slipped around her shoulders, the dampness of her tears seeped through his tunic. He walked with her back to her bur.

Gleineth glanced up in surprise when the door opened. She started to step forward, but paused.

"Leave us," Brenwyn ordered quietly.

As the door closed, Brenwyn sat on the bench and pulled Cyndra onto his knees. He did not try to comfort her with words. He could not promise her it would be all right.

"Why is it so wrong?" she whispered as if he had spoken aloud.

He brought her head to rest on his shoulder and smiled as she nestled against him. "I fight with the Jomsvikings. You are an ealdorman's daughter. The two of us being together seems as unlikely and unnatural as the mating of a wolf and a lark."

"I know how they feel. Before last night . . ."

He tipped her face up. "It will not be easy. Everything will be difficult until the English accept their place as a conquered people."

Cyndra winced. Coming to her feet, she put her hand on the open doors of her bed. "You said you would explain why you were here at Manor Darburgh," she whispered.

"I was sent to learn more about this area so we could know what we faced when we were ready to attack."

"That I guessed, but you speak English as if you were born here. Your name is of this country, not of Jylland."

He nodded grimly. "I was born in the Danelaw. My father, Gunnar Arison, wed an Englishwoman. It was my mother who gave me my name."

"Brenwyn Gunnarsson? Your father's name was Gunnar?"

"As our son will be called Brenwynsson." As he drew her back beside him, his hand settled on her abdomen. "Mayhap even now, Cyndra, he sleeps here."

"I think you are overly optimistic." Cyndra blushed. "I still do not understand how you came to be a Jomsviking."

"In my eighth year, my family was slain along with almost everyone else in our village."

"Slain?"

"Massacred by order of Ethelred, who wished to rid the Danelaw of the Norse." His hands clenched into fists. "I was hunting in the forest, but saw the smoke. By the time I returned to the village, my father was the only one in my family still alive. He had watched my mother raped by the English soldiers before they sent her to die in our burning house."

Cyndra swallowed the bile rising from her cramped stomach. When his gaze turned to her, he kissed her as if he could heal his grief with her love. She stroked his cheek, wishing she knew the words to banish this pain she had not guessed he carried within his heart.

"All your family gone," she whispered. "How could you endure that?"

He looked at the bed, but she knew he was not seeing anything but the past. "I mourned, then went on with my life, determined to fulfill the vow I had made to my dying father."

"For vengeance?"

"Yes."

She shivered at the frigid sound of that single word. He needed say nothing more, for that one word told her everything she needed to know about this man to whom her heart begged to belong. The gentle lover was only one facet of him. The savage warrior who would accept nothing but utter defeat of the English was a part of him as well.

"I left England," he continued in the same taut voice, "and journeyed to Jomsburg on the Oder to learn to become a Jomsviking. It was very different from the life my father had intended for me, for, even at that young age, I had been told that my family and the family of Freydis Bjarnisdottir hoped for us to become betrothed and live in their village."

"Betrothed? To Freydis Bj—Bjar—"

The barest hint of a smile tipped his lips. "Freydis Bjarnisdottir. It was decided between our parents only the day before the attack; so Freydis and her family, who had lived in another village, died along with our neighbors."

With a sob, she hid her face against his shoulder. "I wish the Vikings had never come to England."

"Nothing can change the past, Cyndra." He stroked her back. "I take comfort in knowing that my father found a place of glory in Valhalla—"

"Where?"

"Odin's hall in Asgard."

"I still don't understand," she whispered, for she understood too little now.

"Asgard is what you would call *heaven*. The bravest warriors are admitted to Odin's hall as a reward for their bravery. My father would have gained admittance for his valiant resistance."

"And in knowing that your enemies fall before you?" she asked, raising her head.

His hands captured her face between them. "A death-vow cannot be forgotten. As I struggled to become a warrior and then a Jomsviking, I remembered that each day." He released her as he slid up his left sleeve to reveal a jagged scar below his elbow.

"I needed only look here to remind myself of how my blood flowed to mingle with my father's as he died."

She drew his sleeve back down. "Do you have your vengeance now, or will nothing but your death satisfy it?"

"My vengeance will be complete when England— all of England—swears fealty to my king. That is why when the chance came to return to England in the service of King Swein, I did not hesitate to be among those who repaid Ethelred for his bestial attacks on innocent people in the Danelaw."

"I understand." That was not a lie. For the first time, she could comprehend why the Vikings' attacks had been so vicious in recent years. "But why did you come here?"

"With Morcar's incompetence, it did not take long for me to become commander of the *fyrd*. That gave me access to other burghs. I have fulfilled my duties to Thevkil."

She flinched again at the name she had learned to despise.

"You must make your decision, Cyndra. If you decide you want to be mine, there can be no turning back. If you want to be Morcar's, I will send you to him today."

She closed her eyes. If only it were that simple, but one thing she was certain of. Opening her eyes, she looked up at his stern face. "I want to be with you. Just do not expect this will be easy for me. I never considered changing the life I have known as Lady Cyndra, daughter of Ealdorman Edgar."

"You will be Cyndra Edgarsdottir in the way of my people. Is it so different?"

With an unsteady smile, she nodded. "Yes, it is incredibly different. I will try."

"I shall do all I can to be patient with you." He held out his hand. "Take this, and wear it."

She lifted the gold chain and its amulet. The gilded bronze was a narrow wedge that flared in two directions. "What is it?"

"The symbol of Thor's hammer. Under this sign, all are married and build their homes together as we will be once all the arrangements can be made."

"Brenwyn, I—"

With a smile that brooked no protests, he took it and hooked it around her neck. "Wear it, so all may know you are mine."

An icy shiver of premonition slithered along her as she watched her past being wrenched away. There would be no return to what she had been. Around her neck, she wore the symbol of her most traitorous and loving act.

So far.

Cyndra ignored her trembling fingers as she adjusted the silken veil that draped over her hair. She never had touched silk before Brenwyn gave her this fabric which he had brought back to Manor Darburgh for her. The Vikings who traded with the Rus far to the east had purchased this material from traders who had traveled across great deserts even farther to the east. With each motion, it shimmered in the morning sunshine.

"You have many new things to learn, milady," he had teased her when he had given her this veil. "The English have clung to their island while the

Norse have sailed every sea in search of trade and land."

She did not recall what she had said in return, but she remembered his sweet kisses that had drawn them back into the bed they shared whenever he was within the burgh. In the past two months, he had been called away again and again to oversee the subjugation of these hills in the heart of England. Summer was beginning to fade, and the long-awaited wedding was finally about to be held.

Nothing had startled Cyndra more than how easily the residents of Manor Darburgh learned to accept these new ways. In whispers, the ceorls had told her the first week after the Jomsvikings' foray against Manor Darburgh that they would support anything she decided.

It was from the ceorls that she learned what happened the night the Jomsvikings had come here. Brenwyn had appeared before the gate and hailed the guard. Recognizing Brenwyn, the guard had opened the gate. The manor had been taken that bloodlessly.

But there were changes. The Jomsvikings wore trousers under their tunics instead of stockings. At their waists, belts held their knives and the scabbard for their long swords. Many wore a small amulet in the shape of the one Brenwyn had given her. Woven fancywork brightened their drab tunics.

Cyndra was not surprised to see the women adding bits of colorful material to their gowns. When one ceorl was given a dress in the Norse style, others decided to copy its slender-waisted style. She was not one of them, for she could not give up all that she had been.

Bits of the Norse language became part of everyday conversation. At first, she recognized only names during the meal conversations at the high table. By the end of a fortnight, she was able to discern phrases. Brenwyn was adamant that she learn to speak his language. In their bur, he taught her words of love when he held her in his arms.

A knock sounded on Cyndra's door. She whirled, the veil floating about her like a glossy cloud.

Gleineth opened the door and said, "She is ready, milord."

With the smile that he always wore when Gleineth addressed him with that title, Brenwyn stepped inside. He glanced at Gleineth, and she bowed her head before leaving.

He held out his hands. When Cyndra placed hers on his, he said, "You look so beautiful, milady."

"Thank you." She stared at him.

His burgundy tunic was decorated with silver at the hem and around the neck. A brooch of twisted silver and gold closed his cloak, and broad bands of gold marked the strength of his arms. A gold chain was a bright slash against his ebony hair. At his waist was the sword he called Marr, a name he told her was meant to bring fame to the weapon and its wielder. She had been surprised that the Vikings were sentimental about their swords, giving each an identity of its own.

When he sat on the bed, lifting her up to sit beside him, she laughed and said, "Brenwyn, we should think of our wedding ceremony and feast before we think of the pleasure to follow."

His kiss was swift and left her heart beating as rapidly. "I like the course of your thoughts, but mine are on this gift that Geoor brought for us. It is right that you and I should be alone to open it." He placed a small package wrapped in buckskin in her hands.

"A gift?" Her smile faded as she recalled that Geoor had captured the neighboring Manor Tiwburgh. She did not want some trinket that had belonged to that thane.

Brenwyn put his hand over hers. "Do not fear, milady. This is not of Manor Tiwburgh. Geoor gives this in the manner of the people of Jylland."

She untied the string and unfolded the material around the gift. Inside she discovered two small, bronze statues. She examined them. One was clearly female, the second male.

"Who or what are they?"

He laughed and took the two small statues. He put them on a shelf over the bed. "The male is Frey, the most favorable god. He brings crops from the earth and wealth to men. The other is his twin sister Freyja, the loveliest goddess." He tilted her chin so her gaze were held by his. "Geoor gives them to us at our wedding because Frey and Freyja bring fertility to men and women as they do to the earth. Geoor wishes they grant us a son to be named Brenwynsson."

"By all the saints!" she gasped.

"Cyndra!" He took her shoulders and shook her harshly. "Take care what you say. Those who answer Thevkil's orders could ask for your life for such words."

Startled, she took a pair of heartbeats to understand why his eyes were storm dark with fury. "It is no more than a habit."

"Be done with it! I do not wish to watch you die."

She bit back her angry words when she saw the truth in his rigid face. He had been teaching her

Norse ways to protect her from those who would gainsay his plans to make her his wife. But he was asking her to give up everything she was. She could pretend, but she could not turn her back on everything that had been. Lying to him threatened to shatter her heart, but losing him would be far worse. She wished she could give her heart as easily as she gave herself to him.

When he brought her face back to hers, he cupped her chin in his hand. "Never forget there are those all around you who wish to see you dead."

"I know." She knew as well that only Brenwyn stood between her and that death. As the daughter of Ealdorman Edgar of Manor Saeburgh, the "scourge of the northern scourge," as his allies had called him, she should have been put to death without delay. She wished she knew if her family were still alive. Brenwyn had not been able to find out, cut off as he was from his commander.

Standing, he held out his hand to her. "I hope that you will be safer once you are my wife, so let us be married."

"Yes," she whispered as if it were her most precious vow. She put her hand in his as he reached for the door.

It exploded open nearly in their faces. When Brenwyn pushed her behind him at the same moment he reached for his sword, she groped for the knife she kept beside the bed.

"Geoor, what are you doing here now?" he asked, leaving his hand to rest on the hilt. "The wedding ceremony is about to start."

"This was just delivered for you." He held out a rolled piece of buckskin, not meeting Cyndra's eyes. Brenwyn unrolled it and scanned it. His face paled, then reddened, but he only nodded to Geoor. "We will leave right away."

"We?" Geoor swallowed roughly as he glanced at Cyndra and away.

"Yes, we." He stuffed the rolled skin in his belt. "Inform the others."

Geoor nodded, gulped again as he looked at her, then rushed away.

"Are you delaying the wedding again?" she asked as she put her hand on Brenwyn's arm.

"I have no choice."

"Where do you and Geoor go?"

He clasped her shoulders before his fingers slipped up beneath her veil to tangle in her hair. When his lips captured hers, she tasted his desperation.

Pulling back, she gasped, "Brenwyn, what is it? What news did the messenger bring?"

"Not news. A summons to Thevkil the Strong."

"Will you be coming back?"

"Yes, *I* will." He drew her back to him. "But I vow that I shall not leave his stronghold without you."

"Without me?" She gripped the front of his tunic. "You're taking me there?"

"The summons is for Brenwyn Gunnarsson and the daughter of Ealdorman Edgar of Manor Saeburgh."

She shook her head. "No, I can't go there."

"You must. If you obey this order, I will not have to obey his other to put you to death immediately."

"If we wed first—"

"We are to leave without delay."

"But our wedding can be done quickly."

His hands encircled her cheeks. "Don't you understand, Cyndra? Thevkil has ordered your death if I make you my wife." He unrolled the skin and tapped some of the odd symbols. "I misjudged his hatred of your family. Mayhap I can persuade him to change his mind."

She glanced at the many lines of writing on the skin and wondered what else the missive said. What was Brenwyn *not* telling her? As she looked from the message to his strained face, she was not sure she wanted to know.

Eleven

Cyndra clutched the reins of her horse as they passed through the gates of a burgh built by King Ethelred to keep out the Vikings. Now the leader of those raiders, Brenwyn's commander Thevkil the Strong, claimed it as his own.

The journey had been long as they traveled the length of England to the far south, but she had not been in a hurry to see it end. Last night, when they sat around a fire on a deserted heath, she had seen Gleineth's fear glistening in her eyes. She knew her maid feared that Ealdorman Edgar's daughter would not return to Manor Darburgh alive.

This morning, Gleineth's face had been streaked with the stains from her tears. Comforting her allowed Cyndra to hide the truth she had let no one, not even Brenwyn, suspect. She had blamed the bad food along the road for her stomach upset, and neither Brenwyn nor her maid had questioned her, for they had found the food unsettling, too. But she knew it was not so simple. She had counted the weeks and guessed she had conceived almost two months before, mayhap even the first night Brenwyn had shared her bed. How proud he would be if he guessed that he had been right when he'd teased her about his child sleeping within her even then!

In addition to the horses they rode and the one carrying their personal effects, there were two more loaded with booty to be given to Thevkil. She did not ask what those boxes contained, for she feared it could be her life they were buying.

Brenwyn never spoke about how his chieftain would react to his continued plans to marry her, but she sensed that he was unsure. Even though his own father had wed an Englishwoman, she knew this situation was different. Her father was Thevkil's greatest foe. She guessed Brenwyn suspected, as she did, that Thevkil had delayed calling Brenwyn to him in hopes that the marriage had already taken place. Then Brenwyn would have had to kill her. She did not speak of that or of what might await them here.

Inside the burgh, the small community was busy. She quickly noted that, although there was some English being spoken, most people were talking in the Vikings' language. She was surprised how many phrases she recognized.

They rode into a courtyard near steps to the tower. Her gaze rose to the huge stone block. It looked impenetrable, and she wondered how the Vikings had captured it. With a sigh of resignation, she knew it was because many of the *fyrds* of England had run instead protecting their burghs.

"Milady?"

She glanced down at Brenwyn's smile. She put her hands on his shoulders and let him help her from her saddle. As her feet touched the ground, his hands slid from her waist to press her against him. His lips lowered to hers, and she tasted a strange intensity in his kiss.

Her fingers caressed his face. "What is wrong, Brenwyn?"

"I am wondering how my report will be received by Thevkil and if he will reward my men as I hope."

"You have served him well. The whole region around Manor Darburgh belongs to you."

He laughed. "You sound like a practical scribe. I should let you make my report. If I can so impress my enemy, surely that will gain me respect from my chieftain."

"I am not your enemy!"

"No, Cyndra, you are not my enemy, but you would wish to see the Norse gone from England. That you must admit."

"Not aloud, and not here."

With another chuckle, he held out his hand. "Come, milady. We must prepare for meeting Thevkil."

As they entered the keep, with Gleineth following, Cyndra stared at the gray stone. Beneath her feet were rushes. The aroma of herbs rose to combat the mildew and dankness. Tapestries hung on the walls. Dragons flew and brave thanes fought to the death across the woven surfaces. Many of the characters were nearly life-size, and she knew these were fine works only a king could possess.

Brenwyn paused before one. On the Viking *drakkar*, round shields protected the ship's side. Striped sails seemed filled with wind, and scarlet flames billowed from the shore. What could only be the bodies of the raiders' victims were scattered by the fires.

"Why would Thevkil want a tapestry of such carnage in his home?" she whispered.

"This was here. A Jomsviking does not carry tapestries with him when he goes a-viking, Cyndra."

"It's horrible." She was beginning to realize how little she knew of her own world. Now, she was learning ways she knew even less about.

"Come, milady," he urged again. He raised her fingers to his lips before he placed them on his arm once more.

The corridors were filled with warriors who had answered the call of King Swein Forkbeard to conquer England. They shouted greetings to Brenwyn. That these men knew Brenwyn Gunnarsson of Manor Darburgh did not surprise Cyndra. He was a great leader and due this respect.

When he opened a door, she entered luxurious quarters.

Gleineth gasped, "Milady, I have never seen rooms this grand."

Cyndra was ready to agree. Lounging benches were covered with soft material. Two bedchambers opened off the room. The smaller one would be for Gleineth. Cyndra went into the other sleeping chamber and touched the carved wood of the bed columns. "This is beautiful."

He put his arms around her. "This also is of England. It may be an idea we should take back to Manor Darburgh with us. I like this wide bed."

"I thought you enjoyed cuddling close."

"That I do." Loosening her traveling cape, he pushed aside her veil and kissed her throat with his insatiable desire for her. Her breathy moan of delight swirled around them. "Let me prove it to you later. I will be back for you soon." He was gone before she could reply.

Brenwyn, she knew, was pleased to be among his comrades. Yet he was uneasy about the upcoming meeting with his chieftain. She wished he had brought Geoor with him, but the orders had not included Geoor's name, so he had remained behind.

"You should wear your best, milady," Gleineth said, coming into the bedchamber. "Your boxes have been brought here."

"Good." It did not amaze her that the Vikings were as efficient about this as they were about everything else.

"How do you fare, milady?"

"Anxious." She rubbed her hands together. "I will be glad when we can return to Manor Darburgh." She laughed tersely. "I never thought I would speak those words."

"That is not what I meant."

Cyndra glanced at her maid and away. She should have guessed that Gleineth would come to suspect what she did, but she must not speak of her inkling that she was pregnant. She wanted to caution Gleineth to say nothing in Brenwyn's hearing, but she could not without explaining why.

And she was unsure of that herself. She should be thrilled to have found such happiness in Brenwyn's arms. That their passion could bring the promise of more joy should be perfect.

She wished she could believe that. One of the casualties of Brenwyn's deception had been her trust—in him and in herself. She had been so certain he was a man like her father, a man she could trust without question. Then he had revealed how he had betrayed her so completely.

Mayhap he still was. She longed to believe his soft words of affection were honest. Mayhap they were, but how could she be certain when he was trying to change everything she was? The endless circle of questions led only to more disquiet.

Gleineth remained oddly silent as Cyndra dressed in the gown she should have worn to her wedding to Brenwyn. A shiver ached across her shoulders. The gown she had brought to Manor Darburgh for her wedding to Morcar she had worn to celebrate Brenwyn's capture of the burgh. Now she was wearing the dress she would have worn to her wedding with Brenwyn to what she feared might be her death.

The door opened, and she gasped. Brenwyn was again the fierce warrior he had been when she was brought to him as his captive. She stared in awe. His leather-trimmed mail jerkin was worn over a short tunic. Heavy boots protected his legs. Slashed leather strips covered his shoulders, and along his upper arm were bands of gold as wide as her palm. His weapons hung from his belt, and he wore a metal helmet. In his left hand was the deadly axe that could sever a man's head from his shoulders in one swing.

His eyes narrowed as he appraised her. She wondered what he sought, for these garments were her best. Silently he held out his hand to her. His grim expression daunted her.

"Brenwyn?" she asked, not sure what else to say.

"No questions now. Come with me." His clipped voice allowed for no discussion.

She placed her trembling fingers on his. As he led her out, she glanced at Gleineth. Her maid was wide-eyed as she sank to a bench, her hands clasped in prayer. Cyndra knew Gleineth feared that her lady would not return.

As she did. She was terrified of meeting Thevkil, whose reputation named him a merciless killer.

Brenwyn kept Cyndra close as they went down the stairs and through the crowded passages. Men paused to stare at her. He was glad she could not understand their lusty comments. More than once, he saw her glance at him, but pretended to be oblivious to the tension surrounding them.

Near the doorway to a well-guarded room, he turned her to face him. "Walk behind me. Your status, until Thevkil changes it, is a slave. Do not speak. To do so without my permission might bring about your death. Do nothing without my permission." He brushed the back of his hand against her cheek, wishing he could take her into his arms and protect her from what awaited within. "Trust me, Cyndra."

Her wide eyes showcased her fear. "I will do as you say."

"And trust me?"

She glanced past him, and he did not need to hear her answer. She could trust Ceorl Brenwyn, but not Brenwyn Gunnarsson.

He stepped around the guard at the door and raised his axe. He struck the door with its handle. It swung open. He entered, not turning to see if Cyndra followed. She knew he was her only ally in this room.

At the far end of the chamber was a throne. Its back was carved with Ethelred's emblems, but the battle banners of the hapless English king were gone. Along the walls stood Thevkil's best warriors.

He looked at the man seated on the throne. Thevkil wore a cloak of royal purple trimmed with silver embroidery. His pale yellow hair fell to his shoulders and was held back by a golden circlet. An unruly beard covered his massive chest.

As Brenwyn crossed the narrow room, every man watched. Not him, but Cyndra. He fought to ignore them. When Thevkil's eyes drilled him like beams of fire, they cut through him. Brenwyn had come to Thevkil to learn when Thevkil was serving with the legendary Erik the Red before Erik's banishment from Jylland for murder.

For all that Brenwyn Gunnarsson had accomplished in England, Thevkil would take credit. That did not upset Brenwyn. All he wanted was to receive word that Manor Darburgh and Cyndra were his.

Brenwyn dropped to his knees, glancing back to be certain Cyndra did the same. He was ordered to rise. He did, glad that she did not move.

Cyndra doubted she could move. Fear riveted her to the floor as she listened to Thevkil's deep voice. She understood little of what he said and Brenwyn replied. Her Norse vocabulary was of things of the hall, and they spoke of war.

She almost missed Brenwyn's order for her to stand. Hiding her fright, she walked to him. He took her arm and pushed her to her knees again as if she were his slave.

Fingers under her chin tilted her face to regard a man who was more than a decade older than Brenwyn. All the terror she had known dimmed as she faced Thevkil the Strong. Her earliest memories were of hearing tales of his savagery as he murdered and robbed and abducted women to be his thrall-concubines. Then, before she had met Morcar, her image of evil had worn this man's face.

She fought to keep her expression vacuous. She did not want him to guess at the depths of her fear or her hatred, but she doubted she could hide the truth when her eyes met his piercing blue ones.

He glanced at Brenwyn and said something. Brenwyn answered, but all she understood were her own name and her father's.

At the mention of her father, Thevkil stared at her, but she held her chin high. Father never cowered before the Norse threat. Neither would she.

One eyebrow raised as he made another comment to Brenwyn. To this, Brenwyn did not reply. Brenwyn frowned, and fear coursed through her again. Something was not right.

Thevkil tightened his grip on her face as he pulled her veil. from her hair. She did not dare to protest as it ripped and her hair billowed around her face. His painful hold on her face kept her from looking at Brenwyn.

She was raised to her feet and turned about in a slow circle. For a second, her eyes met Brenwyn's. When she saw his tight mouth, she was certain something was terribly wrong.

A man standing near the throne made a comment, and the others laughed. She understood enough to know that he had made a very crude jest about her father. A single glance from Thevkil silenced the amusement as his heavy hand shoved her to her knees once more.

Thevkil smiled as he spoke again to Brenwyn. When Brenwyn retorted with anger, Thevkil sat on his stolen throne and repeated the same phrases. Brenwyn's face flushed with fury.

Thevkil gave a sharp order, and another man stepped forward. Thevkil motioned to her.

Cyndra cried out in shock with the man grasped her arms and jerked her to her feet. He pushed her face back and stared at her with a triumphant smile.

She did not lower her eyes as she tried to figure out who he was and why he was holding her like this.

He was a homely man with the scars of pox and battle. His hair hung, unwashed, along his back. As close as she was to him, she could tell it was not the only part of him that rarely came into contact with water. That was unusual for Vikings.

She shrieked as he forced her mouth under his. She struggled to escape. Her hand rose. He caught it, and she screamed Brenwyn's name. When he ran his hands along her as if he were a favorite lover, she heard loud voices.

Brenwyn's and Thevkil's.

Thevkil snapped a word, and the man released her with obvious reluctance.

She started to run to Brenwyn, but he held up his hand. "Stay where you are, Cyndra."

"Brenwyn—"

He frowned at her.

"As you wish, milord." She knelt again. She rested on her heels as she stared at her clenched hands. Her knuckles were bleached white.

Brenwyn did not look at her as he resumed the heated debate with Thevkil.

When Thevkil nodded with obvious reluctance, a murmur of amazement circled the room.

Brenwyn came over to her, and she asked, "What is wrong?"

"Oleif, because of his higher rank, has demanded I turn over my booty to him. That includes you."

"Oleif?"

He glanced at the man who had kissed her. "If I wish to retain my share of the victory spoils, I must challenge him in hand-to-hand battle."

"No, Brenwyn!" She knew enough of Viking ways

to know such a battle would last until one man was dead.

"I vow to you that I will not let you go to Oleif, Cyndra, as your father sent you to Morcar."

Her face grew cold as she glanced from him to the man Thevkil had given her to. She stiffened her shoulders. "May your arm be strong and your eye keen. Come back bathed in honor and the blood of your enemies."

For the first time, he smiled. "Your admonition reminds me of one the women of Jylland speak to their men as they leave to go a-viking."

"I repeat Father's orders to his men."

"Wise words which I shall heed."

"Come forward, Englishwoman," Thevkil ordered in English.

She glanced at Brenwyn, then obeyed. Fighting her quivering knees, she walked to where Thevkil was sitting on his throne.

"You are Lady Cyndra, daughter of the Ealdorman Edgar?"

She nodded, wondering why he was asking her when he must know.

"Answer me, Englishwoman."

"I am Lady Cyndra, daughter of the Ealdorman Edgar." Another low rumble raced through the room.

"I had heard," Thevkil said as he drew his knife and pared his nails, "that you were sent to wed Morcar of Manor Darburgh."

"That is true."

"His death will prevent your marriage."

She gasped, "Morcar is dead?" She looked back at Brenwyn. Was this the first he had heard of Morcar? She could not tell because his face was again without expression.

Thevkil smiled. "You show more pleasure than despair at such news, milady." Not giving her a chance to reply, he continued, "Your father was a most worthy opponent when we last met. His *fyrd* forced us to retreat three summers ago. Do you recall that, milady?"

"Yes, I recall that." Meeting his eyes evenly, she said, "He spoke of your skill that was almost a match for his."

"Almost?" He grasped her arm, tugging her to her knees in front of the throne. Ignoring Brenwyn's protest, he placed the flat of knife against her neck. No one spoke as he moved the knife around her throat. The sharp blade nicked her skin, but she bit her lip to restrain a sob of pain.

He laughed. "You are not without courage yourself, Lady Cyndra, daughter of Ealdorman Edgar. His spirit will be granted admittance to Valhalla, although he was English. Do you think he will find welcome among his enemies?"

"If entering Valhalla requires courage and wisdom, my father will be granted a seat close to Odin." She struggled to speak past her horror. Father was dead? She did not want to believe it, but Thevkil's words confirmed her worst fears. Father was dead. What of Sigestan? Did her brother still live? She did not dare to ask. If Sigestan had escaped, she must not focus Thevkil's vengeance on him.

"Is that so?" Thevkil chuckled. "You come from a valiant burgh. The *fyrd* stood by your fallen father until they, too, died. I watched the walls razed, so no English burgh can be raised there again against us."

Tears burned in her throat. Keeping her head high prevented them from falling along her face. She would not weep before this beast who was enjoying her grief. She would not!

Had Brenwyn known Saeburgh was destroyed? No, he would have told her gently, sparing her this barbaric announcement. She wanted his arms around her now. His rigid face warned that he was furious that Thevkil was being so cruel. But Thevkil was his leader, his mentor, the man he might still aspire to be. How could her heart long to belong to a man who was a part of this savagery?

Thevkil tilted his knife beneath her jaw. "Your father will stop us no more. He refused to plead to be spared."

She understood the threat he did not speak. She would not beg for her life either. "You do me honor, milord, with your respect for my father."

" 'Bathed in honor and with the blood of your enemies' were your words to Brenwyn Gunnarsson, milady."

"The same my father would have held close to his heart while he defended what is his."

Thevkil's gaze bore into her. "It is foolish to allow one of Ealdorman Edgar's progeny to live, for such a child might have the wisdom and wiliness of its father. That you have proven already, milady. We need subjects who obey, not plot insurrection behind such loveliness that it twists a man's mind from his duty."

"I understand, milord." She kept emotion from her voice. All feeling was gone, seared away by her terror. Only regret remained, regret that the time she had had with Brenwyn had been so short. "I ask that you choose a quick death for me so I do not shame my father's memory."

He roared with laughter. He grasped a glass from a servant and took a long drink of it to drown his amusement. When he could speak, it was no longer in her language.

Cyndra watched as Brenwyn walked toward her. She tried to read his expression, but it told her nothing. Had he been chosen to be her executioner? Mayhap Thevkil demanded this of Brenwyn to test his fealty.

Brenwyn took Cyndra's hand, startling her. And Thevkil, who surged to his feet. He threw the goblet to the floor. It shattered, splashing wine on her. He shouted something, his amusement once again rage.

Bowing his head, Brenwyn tugged on her hand. She went with him, expecting the thrust of a knife in her back at any moment. When they left the room, she started to speak. Brenwyn scowled her to silence.

Perplexed, she said nothing as he led her back to their rooms. When he closed the door and dropped the bar, she gasped, "Brenwyn, I thought Thevkil intended to slay me."

"He did intend to see you dead."

"Then what—?"

"Not even Thevkil can set himself above the law." He drew her down to sit on a bench. "I have asked that my claim be discussed at the Thing."

"What thing?"

He smiled. "The Thing is our meeting of justices, where disputes are settled."

"Thevkil agreed?" She had never imagined that Thevkil the Strong would obey any laws but his own.

"It is my right." Brenwyn did not add that Thevkil

had urged him to forget Cyndra and the poor manor. Thevkil had offered him richer prizes if he would let Oleif have Cyndra, but he had demanded to keep what he had won. Thevkil's plans to torment the daughter of his greatest enemy must never come to pass.

"Milady!" Gleineth rushed from the small chamber and fell to her knees in front of Cyndra. Hiding her face in Cyndra's gown, she wept. "I thought I would never see you again. Thank you, milord, for protecting us."

"Not all of us," Cyndra whispered, and he put his arm around her shoulders to find them quivering like a ripped sail in a high wind.

"What do you mean?" her maid gasped.

Taking Gleineth's hands, she whispered, "Father is dead."

"No, milady!" She moaned and sat back on her heels, rocking with her grief.

Brenwyn nearly recoiled when Cyndra turned to him. The sorrow that haunted him was diminished by the agony in her eyes, raw and fresh. When he put his hand up to draw her lips to his, she edged back.

"Did you know?" she whispered.

"Did I know your father was dead?" He shook his head. "I told you that I did not know who lived and who had died."

"Did you know that Manor Saeburgh was the focus of Thevkil's fury?"

The strength that had steadied him during his argument with his chieftain faltered at her quiet question. The truth would be rubbing salt in her open wounds. Folding her hands between his, he said,

"Sweet one, you know that any knowledge I had of Thevkil's plans I had to keep to myself."

She slipped her hands out of his as tears flashed silver along her face. Rising, she did not speak as she walked into the larger bedchamber and closed the door.

Brenwyn stood. When Gleineth put her hand on his arm, keeping him from following Cyndra, he shook her off. She gripped his sleeve.

"Milord," she whispered, "do not go after her."

"She is distraught. She should not be alone."

"She shan't be alone." She edged back a step, moving between him and the door. "I shall be with her."

"Gleineth, get out of my way so I can—"

"So you can what?" she asked as if he were a ceorl she was about to chide again. "Haven't you done enough, milord? How many more times can you ask her to believe you when you have betrayed her on every turn?"

He did not answer as she opened the door and went in. He cursed when he heard the bar fall heavily, locking him out. When he raised his fist, ready to slam it against the door, he hesitated.

How many more times can you ask her to believe you when you have betrayed her on every turn?

He walked away from the door, because he knew the answer to that. A death-vow had brought him to this place at this time, and he could not turn his back on that vow until he had fulfilled it. Yet, for the first time, he realized how high the cost of his vengeance could be and how impossible it was for him to change now.

Even for this chance at love.

Twelve

"I don't know!"

When Gleineth recoiled from her harsh words, Cyndra wished she could retract them, even though they were the truth. She did not know when they were leaving this horrible place. How could she? Brenwyn had not been within these rooms for the past six days, and she had not been out of them. The sole time she had seen him was when he rode out of the courtyard below alone. She had no idea where he might be bound or why he had abandoned her here.

Her grief that had changed to fury had become frustration, then sorrow again. She had lost her home and her father. Mayhap even Sigestan. She now feared she had lost Brenwyn. Not even Gleineth's calm words that Brenwyn should have been honest with her eased her heartache. How could he when he was bound by his oath to obey his commander's orders? How could he when he knew, as she did, that she would have sought a way to warn her father?

"Forgive me," she whispered, both to her maid and her father. "I am not angry with you, Gleineth."

"We should leave."

"I know."

"If milord wishes to remain—"

She gathered up the tunic she had started for Brenwyn before they left Manor Darburgh. "Do not be silly, Gleineth. We would not get a league alone. No one is safe within England now without a strong sword arm."

A knock came on the outer door. Cyndra glanced at her maid, then nodded.

Gleineth opened the door and murmured something to the person on the other side. When she stepped back, a woman came into the room.

Cyndra stared. She could not help herself. The woman was exquisitely beautiful. Her hair was the spun gold of spring sunshine and her eyes pale blue. She was tall enough to be a Valkyrie. Quickly she looked away, not because of her caller, but because of her own thoughts. Two months ago, she would not have made such a comparison.

"Are you Cyndra, Brenwyn Gunnarsson's thrall-concubine?" the woman asked in unaccented English.

"Yes." She ignored Gleineth's gasp of denial.

"I am Hallgred Bjarnisdottir."

She recognized the name instantly, for she had heard Brenwyn speak it when he spoke of his shattered past and the young girl he had intended to wed. "You must be Freydis Bjarnisdottir's sister."

"You know of Freydis?"

"Brenwyn told me that your parents and his had wanted them to marry." She motioned to a bench.

Hallgred sat, her silk gown whispering with every motion. "I was left without parents and a sister that day. My older brother and his wife took me into their home until I married."

"But didn't you say your name is—"

She laughed lightly. "A Norse woman never forgets her father and keeps his name as hers even when she is wed."

"So it is with English women. My name has always been Cyndra, daughter of Ealdorman Edgar." She chose a bench facing the other woman.

Hallgred glanced at Gleineth. "I came to speak with *you*, Cyndra Edgarsdottir."

When Cyndra dismissed her maid, she knew Gleineth would wait close to the bedchamber door, taking note of every word. She guessed Hallgred Bjarnisdottir would know that, too. She wanted to ask why Hallgred was here, but needed to guard every word. She understood too little of Norse ways.

"Who are you?" Hallgred asked so abruptly that Cyndra gasped.

"You know my name."

"I know that, but nothing else. You speak of your father with pride, but who is he?"

For a moment, Cyndra was shocked, then she realized that what was spoken of within Thevkil's council chamber might not be repeated throughout the burgh. She folded her hands in her lap and let her chin rise with the pride she had tried to submerge among her father's enemies. "My father, Ealdorman Edgar of Manor Saeburgh, was an advisor to King Ethelred and the bane of the Norse invaders. From him to me comes the blood of the daughters of kings."

"Now I understand." She smiled.

Cyndra did not.

Before she could say that, Hallgred went on, "I had heard that the chieftain refused to grant Brenwyn Gunnarsson permission to wed you. This all makes sense."

"Not to me."

With a laugh, Hallgred leaned forward and patted Cyndra's clenched fingers. "I was born in the Danelaw, so I know well the ways of both Norse and English. They are not so different. Thevkil fears that, by wedding you, Brenwyn will gain status beyond his when the defeat of Ethelred is complete."

"I have no status now. I am no more than a slave."

"Mayhap, but the blood within you cannot be changed, only spilled."

Cyndra's eyes grew wide. Now, she *did* understand. Coming to her feet, she whispered, "But stopping our marriage will change nothing."

"Do not fear. Brenwyn Gunnarsson has announced his determination to make you his wife. Many who owe allegiance to Brenwyn Gunnarsson have taken note of that and have made certain that you will not die at the hands of the chieftain's minions." She stood and smiled. "If they had not, you would be dead now."

"Thevkil is a chieftain. Brenwyn is—"

"Respected by many, who know what he sacrificed to make this foray a success." Her smile faded as she sighed. "While others plied the king with flattery and gained his favor, Brenwyn Gunnarsson lived among those he has the most reason to hate and gave up his chance for advancement. Such a man of honor has many admirers."

Man of honor? How was it that everyone else could believe that, even her heart believed that, but she could not trust him? He was everything she had dreamed of—strong and courageous; but he was a

Viking who had lied to her from the moment they met.

Hallgred must have misread her silence, because she put her hand on Cyndra's arm. "Cyndra Edgarsdottir, I know you grieve the deaths of your family. I know your sorrow, for I have suffered as you do now. Please heed my words, knowing that I speak them because of my admiration for Brenwyn Gunnarsson and all he has done to avenge my family as well as his. He continues to forfeit his chances for the prestige that should rightly be his."

"By wishing to wed me?"

She nodded. "For what he has done, he should be greatly rewarded. He—"

The door to the hallway opened. As Brenwyn walked into the room, his gaze met Cyndra's and he smiled. She wanted to rush to be enfolded to him, but glanced at Hallgred.

His face paled. "Freydis?"

"I am Hallgred Bjarnisdottir."

With a laugh, he said, "By Thor's beard, you look as your sister should have when she was grown. You have changed from the nurseling you were when I last saw you."

"And you have grown to be a man whose deeds are spoken of with pride and awe." She took Cyndra's hand. "I am glad we could meet, Cyndra Edgarsdottir." Putting Cyndra's hand in Brenwyn's, she smiled. "I wish you the happiness I have discovered in the wake of pain."

"Thank you," Cyndra whispered as Brenwyn spoke the same words only a bit louder.

Even as the door was closing behind Hallgred, Brenwyn pulled Cyndra to him and tilted her face beneath his. She did not speak as he searched it with the intensity she sensed all along him. His fingers spread across her cheek like melting butter as his lips brushed hers. She ached for more than this light kiss, but did not want to do anything to cause him to leave again.

He raised his mouth only far enough so he could murmur, "I never knew six days could be so endless, sweet one."

"And six nights without you sleeping beside me."

"Sleeping is something I have not done much of since we last spoke."

"Brenwyn—"

He put his finger to her lips. "Say no more of what we last said to each other in pain and anger. Say instead that you wish to be mine."

"I do wish to be yours."

"My wife?"

She gasped, "But Thevkil ordered—"

"Will you heed Thevkil or your heart?" His hand curved along her breast, and he smiled as her heartbeat throbbed against it. "I have spent the past six days arranging for our marriage to take place."

"We can be prepared to leave for Manor Darburgh within the hour."

He shook his head. "The marriage will take place here."

"Here?"

"Yes." He teased her ear with the tip of his tongue. "Then you and I will be one."

"You and I and . . ." She drew his hand down over her stomach. "And the one within me."

He captured her face between his hands. "A child, Cyndra?"

"*Our* child." When he glanced away, she whispered, "Our child. It cannot be Morcar's. He was so determined that his heir would be legitimate, he stayed away from my bur."

"If I had thought otherwise, I would not have left you there with him."

"You are saying nothing of the child. Are you displeased?"

He laughed. "Sweet one, how could I be displeased? Soon I shall have a son to become a warrior as his father is or a daughter who will be as lovely as her mother and delight me with grandchildren."

"Grandchildren? Our little one is yet unborn, and you already are planning to be a grandsire."

"When, Cyndra?"

"Count the days from the night you first came to me, Brenwyn Gunnarsson."

He chuckled. "And you told me I was being too prideful."

"You were."

He kissed her with all his longing, then held out his hand. "Let us get married. Then we shall celebrate this wondrous news." His smile became a promise of pleasure. "Together."

"That is the way this little one came into being," she teased as she saw the glimmer of yearning in his expressive eyes.

"Can you think of a better way to share the joy?"

He gave her no chance to answer as he called for Gleineth. When her maid peeked out of her room, he motioned for Gleineth to follow them. He hushed Gleineth before she could ask a single question.

Cyndra was silent as well when Brenwyn led them through empty halls. If someone approached, he took them in a different direction. He must want no one to guess their destination. When he opened a door to a chamber high in the tower, she guessed it once had been a chapel. Nothing remained but the niches for the statues.

"You wish to be married here?" she whispered.

"I thought you would."

She bit her lip to keep from thanking him as a man stepped from the shadows. In her anger at Brenwyn, she had forgotten his kindness. Mayhap he had not told her about the attack on Manor Saeburgh because he wished to spare her from pain as long as possible.

The ceremony was simple. The man held out a stone, which she knew was to represent Thor's hammer, and she knelt beneath it. She fought not to glance up at it in trepidation. As the Norse words were spoken, in her heart came the echo of the ceremony that she had known. The promises of fidelity were the same.

Cyndra looked up when Brenwyn faltered on one answer. He put his hand on her shoulder and motioned for her to rise. "Is something wrong?" she asked.

"I should pay your father a bride-price to prove that I wish to make you a wife, not a thrall-concubine."

She looked at the man with the hammer. Hoping she did not use the wrong words, she said in the Vikings' language, "Brenwyn gave my father his son's life by saving it in battle. That is a bride-price beyond measure."

Brenwyn smiled. "This is true. By my hand, his heir and his daughter were returned to him alive."

The man mumbled something, but continued. Brenwyn took her hand and squeezed it. When the man paused, Brenwyn tugged her into her arms. His mouth captured hers, and she gave herself to the kiss as she wanted to give herself to him.

Gleineth began to congratulate them, but barely had a chance to speak before Brenwyn hurried them out of the room and back through the twisting passages. The grim lines had returned to his face, so Cyndra knew he still worried someone would learn of this secret ceremony.

That solemn expression vanished as soon as he pulled her into their private chamber and closed the door. "Do not shut me out again, sweet one."

"I would like to promise—"

"But milady's temper is a match for any warrior's." Brenwyn laughed and spun Cyndra into his arms which ached for her. "*Milady*. You are mine."

"Hallgred warned me of what you have given up to marry me."

"Nothing of import, and the sweetest prize of all is mine."

His hands moved along her slender body. When she grasped his face, bringing his mouth to hers, he tasted her fevered response. He leaned her back onto the lush bed he had waited so long to share with her. When his fingers lingered over where his child slept, her hand covered his.

"Soon you will feel him kicking," she whispered. "Then, not long after that, you will hold him in your arms."

"Now the only one I want to hold is you, dear wife."

Lifting her mouth for his kiss, she murmured, "Hold me now and forever."

"There is nothing I would rather do."

He reached to draw the bed curtains closed and

smiled at her puzzlement. "I am shutting out the rest of the world."

He gave her no chance to answer as he claimed her soft lips once more. Slowly, but with as much eagerness as the first time he had held her in her bed, he loosened her clothes and tossed them away. He groaned with the undeniable need when she undressed him. His skin craved the soft caress of hers against it.

Her mouth urged him to search more deeply for his delight. His fingers tingled as he touched her. Rolling her atop him, he forgot everything but the tempest that raged within them. He caressed her breasts before bringing them to his mouth. A cry of rapture burst from her lips amid her short breaths, and he pressed her hips to his. He wanted her softness all around him.

Her breath branded him with her fiery need as she writhed against him when she moved to draw him over her. His mouth rediscovered what his eyes could not see in the dusky twilight. Beneath his fingers, her body arched toward him. With a muted chuckle, he pressed her into the mattress. Her mouth surrendered to his assault. As their breaths mingled, his fingers slipped along her legs to stroke her until she shuddered beneath him.

He sought his welcome deep in her body. Her gasps spiraled around him until it became the sweetest song. His hands fisted as he fought his own desire until she quivered around him. As she gasped his name, he gave himself to the ecstasy he never would have to deny himself again, for she was his until death separated them.

He refused to think, in this moment of ultimate delight, how soon that could be.

* * *

At last, they were leaving. Cyndra closed the box and looked around the bedchamber. From the other room, she could hear Gleineth making final preparations. Her maid was as anxious as she was to put Thevkil's burgh behind them.

She frowned. The pile of food packages that Brenwyn had been able to smuggle into their room was small. He had few excuses to go to the kitchens without causing curiosity. They would need more than this to eat until they could get to a village where they could buy food without calling attention to themselves.

Looking down at her simple robes, she drew her traveling cloak over her head. She gazed into the shield on the wall. Yes, she could be mistaken for a ceorl. If she were cautious, she might be able to get more food for them.

She slipped out of the room and along the hallway, hoping nobody saw her. Carefully, she noted the tapestries which would guide her way back. The other times she had come this way, she had been with Brenwyn. It did not take her long to find a doorway leading to one of the courtyards.

Wrapping her mantle around her face, she went into the garden beyond the door. In the heat, many of the flowering bushes had withered. She wandered across the open area toward the kitchen.

Brenwyn confused her. He spoke more and more in the language of his father and urged her to use it herself. If he knew she knew a word in the Norse language, he would not answer her if she used English. He wanted her to become as Norse as he was. Yet he hid their marriage from his commander.

Mayhap he had believed what she did. Thevkil would never accept the daughter of his most hated enemy as Brenwyn's wife. When they returned to Manor Darburgh, things would be better. There no one despised her for choosing Brenwyn over Morcar.

Bird-song interrupted her unhappy thoughts. She looked up into the tree. A hand came from behind her, clamping over her mouth. She tried to pull away, but an arm closed like an iron band around her. She was yanked back against mail.

She could not scream because the hand covered her nose, too. Her vision grew wavy as she fought to breathe. Her cloak was tightened over her face as she was dragged across the courtyard, gasping for air.

A door opened, and she was shoved forward. The door slammed shut. Pushing aside her cloak, she could see nothing. The room was lost to darkness. She took a single step and tripped over something. Mud and water oozed through her dress and dripped from her hands as she pushed herself to her feet. She held out her hands and found the door in three steps. When she ran her hands along it, a splinter sliced into her fingers.

There was no latch.

Checking that it was dry by the door, Cyndra sat with her back against it. For some reason, someone had imprisoned her. Not someone. Thevkil. Had he found out about the wedding?

Drawing up her knees, she placed her head on her arms. She did not chide herself for leaving her rooms and walking into this trap. Thevkil would have abducted her from her rooms. She had made it simpler for him.

She cursed him, then took a steadying breath.

Once Brenwyn discovered she was missing, he would search every room. He would find her. She held onto that thought as a comfort against the darkness.

Every time it seemed happiness might be within their grasp, someone tried to destroy it. She could not dampen the fear that, this time, those who hated them might be successful.

Brenwyn whistled a light tune as he walked through the tower. No one must suspect that last night Cyndra had become his wife and today they were leaving this burgh. He opened the door to their rooms and called, "Cyndra?"

"She is not here, milord." Gleineth frowned as she set a bag on the floor. "I thought she must have gone with you."

"I have just returned." He saw her face blanch, but he said, "Wait here. I will get her and return. Then we will leave."

"Do you think—"

He left before he had to voice one of his thoughts. All led to one conclusion. One he did not like.

He swore as he strode along the hall. She should have known better than to leave their rooms today. As he took the stairs, three at a time, his cape flapped behind him like the wings of a seabird taking flight.

Thevkil glanced up in shock as the door to his audience room opened with a crash. "I was about to send for you, Brenwyn."

"I don't doubt that. Where is Cyndra?" he asked, ignoring the other men in the room.

"Do you speak of Lady Cyndra, the daughter of Ealdorman Edgar . . . or I should I call her Cyndra

Edgarsdottir, your wife?" He came to his feet and scowled.

Brenwyn put his hand on his sword. "You know of our wedding. Do you know as well what has happened to Cyndra?"

"Mayhap."

"I deserve an answer."

Thevkil's frown did not lessen. "Then you shall have one. She is safe. She will remain so while you complete a task for me." He turned to a table where maps were spread out. "News of our victory must be taken to Swein Forkbeard. The messenger must travel through areas still held by the English. You know these English better than any of my other warriors, so you will go."

Brenwyn's eyebrows came together. "I have always obeyed your orders."

"Save for when I told you not to marry Cyndra, daughter of Ealdorman Edgar."

"You ordered me to postpone our wedding and leave Manor Darburgh to come here without delay. Both orders I obeyed."

Snickers came from the other men, and Thevkil's face reddened with fury.

"So, why do you hold my woman?" Brenwyn asked.

"Why not?" He sat and stretched out his legs in front of him. "You have spent much time among these English. Is it only your wife's beauty that turns your head?"

This was an insult Brenwyn had not expected. He had fought beside Thevkil since he had gone to Jylland. While his chieftain had enjoyed his home there, Brenwyn had endured acting as Morcar's ceorl. The victory to the north came from his work.

But the simple act of marrying Cyndra damned him as a traitor.

He unbuckled his sword belt and tossed it at Thevkil's feet. His voice was as cold as a night in the land of the Lapps. "I return my sword of fealty to you, for it seems you no longer deem me worthy of wearing it."

Thevkil erupted from his chair. He took a step toward Brenwyn, then paused. Bending, he picked up the belt and drew the broad blade. He turned it in his hand and walked toward Brenwyn.

Brenwyn watched as his commander advanced on him with his own sword. Even when the blade was held up before him, he did not flinch. He had fought one battle to have Cyndra. He would not back down from this one.

For a long minute, no one moved. Then Thevkil twisted the blade and offered its hilt. "Take your sword of fealty, Under-Chieftain Brenwyn Gunnarsson."

Gasps echoed through the room at his sudden promotion to Thevkil's second-in-command. Brenwyn stood still. He would not accept honors at the cost of Cyndra's life.

Thevkil swore a violent curse. His bitten-off order sent one of his men racing from the room. He walked back to his chair. Leaning on the sword that bit into the grout between the stones in the floor, he laughed.

Brenwyn arched his eyebrows as he relaxed slightly. He recognized that laugh. Thevkil admired Brenwyn's stubborn courage that matched his own.

When the door opened, Cyndra entered. Brenwyn

watched in silence as she crossed the floor as tranquilly as if nothing had been amiss.

"Here is your woman." Thevkil smiled. "Unharmed, as I told you."

"I see that," Brenwyn answered tersely. He saw the filth on her clothes and wondered what she had suffered.

Thevkil picked up a packet from the table. He tossed it to Brenwyn, who caught it easily. Putting the sword back into its scabbard, he threw that in Brenwyn's direction as well.

"You have your mission, Underchieftain Brenwyn Gunnarsson. Take your wife with you to deliver my report to Swein, for she has no place here. I hope you do not come to regret the decisions you made here today."

Brenwyn glanced from Thevkil's smile to Cyndra, whose face was the shade of the stones. By Thor's hammer, he had let his commander twist his words so that now he had no choice but to take Cyndra to Swein Forkbeard's fortress. He could not go first to Manor Darburgh, where he could leave her in safety. Or was there any place in England where Cyndra would be safe now?

She would be safe with him. That he vowed. *I will make no vows I may be unable to keep.* He hoped his own words would not come back to haunt him.

Thirteen

Brenwyn watched Cyndra carefully as the day faded toward twilight. This journey was demanding too much of her. A fortnight ago, two of their horses had gone lame, so they walked, leading the remaining one. Gleineth had tried to help him persuade Cyndra to ride, but Cyndra insisted walking was safer for her and the unborn child.

Mayhap it had been, but as she thickened with the growing child, he wished he could send her to the safety of Manor Darburgh. The journey had lengthened threefold when he learned that King Swein had moved his court within the borders of the Danelaw for the coming of winter.

He was pleased to see a farmstead in a forest clearing. Any signs of Brenwyn's allegiance were hidden among their packs as they assumed the identities of a ceorl and his woman and servant. Their tale of being forced from their home by the Vikings brought them sympathy that made Cyndra uncomfortable. She did not like accepting the food from those who thought they were aiding refugees.

He cared only that she had good food and a place to sleep at the end of the day. Soon they were being welcomed by Oswiu the farmer, his wife Eadburh, and their daughter Deira.

Cyndra was too tired to think of their lies as she accepted Eadburh's invitation to sit by the hearth. It had started to rain at sunrise, and they were soaked and stank of wet wool.

It was wondrous to be in a house again. The nights they had spent in byres with the hushed sounds of the animals were better than the ones in the forest.

She and Gleineth helped Eadburh prepare the venison stew for their meal as Deira brought mead for her father and Brenwyn. Oswiu spoke of the lack of news about Edmund Ironside's efforts to wrest his father's kingdom back from the Vikings. Rumor suggested that Ethelred sought seclusion in a monastery, abandoning his subjects as he sought to free himself of the sin that had brought the curse of the Norse upon England.

"Let them speak of war," Eadburh said as she stirred some carrots into the stew. "I would rather speak of my hopes for good weather for Deira's betrothal to our neighbor's son. It is a fine match."

"And Deira is pleased?" asked Cyndra.

"She is most pleased. You sound sad. Surely you cannot be displeased with your husband. He dotes on you."

She glanced at Gleineth, who said, "She is not thinking of herself but of a lady I served. How sorrowful she was to wed the man her parents chose!"

"That is how it is for the thanes and their ladies. For them, there is a life of luxury and little joy." She smiled, her few remaining teeth sparkling in the firelight. "We may be poor, but we have happiness, don't we? Who is the richer?"

"I hope you are right," Cyndra said.

"She is," Gleineth added when Eadburh looked at her with curiosity.

Cyndra said little during their evening meal. Fatigue weighed like a smith's anvil around her shoulders. When Oswiu offered them the lean-to connected to the house, she started to protest their generosity.

Brenwyn hushed her. "I need to map out our route for the morrow," he said quietly.

She nodded. His maps were covered with words in the Norse language. If this family chanced to see them, it could cause trouble.

Gleineth spread their blankets on the floor, saying nothing. While Cyndra watched Brenwyn check his maps before unlacing his garters to remove his boots, she was as silent.

Sitting on a blanket beside the small window, Brenwyn drew her next to him. "It is all right, Cyndra."

"I am tired of lying all the time."

"You are not lying. You are letting them keep their assumptions unchanged. It protects them and us."

When his lips captured hers, she sensed his sorrow at causing her pain. He leaned her back on their makeshift bed, and she drew him with her, wanting him to heal the wounds that festered in her heart.

Suddenly, he yelped and pulled away.

"What is wrong?" she gasped.

With a grin, he said, "I think Farmer Oswiu's roof has a leak. That drip down my back was cold." He slid the blanket away and brought her with him. "You must stop worrying so much about what other people think and get some sleep. It is late, and I fear the weather will be no better tomorrow."

"Yes," she agreed, quickly. She wanted to savor

being in Brenwyn's arms and put everything else aside. "Good night."

When he drew her head down to rest on his shoulder, her fingers reached across his chest to be enfolded in his hand as she fell asleep amid the perfect dream of happiness.

A noise brought Gleineth abruptly awake. Her ears strained so hard, she could detect the sound of her own heartbeat. Just as she was telling herself she had imagined the sound, she heard it again.

She crawled to the door and opened it to peek out. Angry voices pushed into the room as strangers burst into the other room. Their dress labeled them as Vikings.

She scurried away from the door. Shaking her lady awake, she whispered, "Milady, where is milord?"

"Brenwyn is—" Cyndra blinked groggily, then realized he was not beside her. "What is wrong, Gleineth?"

"There are Vikings out in the main room."

"Vikings?"

Before Gleineth could stop her, Cyndra went to the door and peered out of it. A trio of men stood in the middle of the room. None of them was Brenwyn, and none of them was a Viking, although they wore chain mail and Norse helmets. Who were they? Outlaws who were using this guise to terrorize their victims?

Where was Brenwyn?

"They are not Jomsvikings," she whispered. "What they are saying is just nonsense."

"Are you sure?"

"Yes," she said, although she was not. One thing

she *was* certain of. "We are in danger, Gleineth, very bad danger."

Taking her arm, Gleineth tugged her to the small window at the back of the lean-to. Together they lifted a wooden block to set beneath it so they could climb out. She did not hesitate as she squeezed through the narrow opening.

The jar as she hit the ground sent an ache through her whole body, but she did not cry out. Rising, she held out her hands to Gleineth.

"Run, milady!"

The door to the lean-to crashed open. She tried to climb back in, but Gleineth shoved her away. She whirled and ran toward the trees. She could not help if she were captured, too.

When she reached the brush at the edge of the clearing, she paused. What could she do? She had no weapon. The false Vikings had knives. A scream ravaged the night. A woman shrieking in terror.

Before she could rush back, a hand caught her arm. She was whirled to see Brenwyn's grim face. He drew her more deeply into the underbrush and squatted as he looked back at the house.

"Gleineth is still inside," she gasped. "With the false Jomsvikings."

"False Jomsvikings?" He nodded. "So, that is their ploy. When I heard noise out here, I came out to investigate. I chased one man into the woods."

"While he drew you away, the others attacked."

"You English are endlessly wily."

"These are outlaws. Don't confuse them with law-abiding English."

"I shan't." His jaw tightened. "It's time to teach them a lesson that they are not wily enough."

"What do you have planned?"

"Victory with your help, milady."

Another scream came from the house. "Tell me what I must do."

Oswiu watched as the well-armed man advanced on his daughter. He could not aid her for he was being held by the other two men. His wife had been knocked aside when she tried to help Deira, and now she lay on the floor, unmoving, with a trickle of blood at her mouth. Gleineth crouched beside her. As the man reached for Deira, a knock sounded.

The leader of the three hissed a warning as he went to the door. Despite his threats, it took a knife to Deira's throat to keep Oswiu from shouting a warning to Cyndra. What was she doing back here?

"Is Farmer Oswiu in?" Cyndra asked, trying to appear as if nothing were amiss. "I am Cyndra, and I have a message for him."

"He is within, woman." His tongue slid like a slimy slug along his mouth. He stepped into the doorway.

She gasped as lamplight glittered off his battered mail. Then she forced a seductive smile on her lips. "Jomsvikings! I have heard much of you."

"We are the world's finest warriors!" boasted the man.

"That is not all I have heard. I have heard you are as accomplished in other ways. A real man it takes to conquer an empire. A real man it takes to satisfy a woman."

He pulled her to him, and she prayed he was too filled with lust to notice the thickening at her waist. She paid no attention to Deira's cry. He gripped the front of her gown, but she did not succumb to panic. Instead, she smiled and patted his fingers, keeping them away from her.

"Not here," she whispered. "My man is jealous, and I do not wish him to know. Let us go out in the darkness."

"The floor here—"

"I know a place where you can teach me all you know." She ran her fingertip along his ear, trying to quell the disgust in her stomach.

He laughed. "Wait here with the prisoners," he ordered the others. When they started to protest, he said, "You can have your turn next."

Her stomach threatened to betray her. If their plan went awry . . . No, she could not think of that.

He dragged her only a few steps out into the night before he clamped his mouth over hers. When she stiffened, he taunted, "Changed your mind, Cyndra? It is too late. There are three of us willing to accept your proposition. We—" He dropped into a pile at her feet.

Brenwyn wiped his knife on the man's tunic and cursed. Pulling off the Norse helmet, he snarled, "May you rot for robbing the dead." He looked at Cyndra, who stood with her arms wrapped around herself. "Did he hurt you?"

"No!" She flung her arms around him to be held by his comfortingly familiar body. As he caressed her, she told him of the situation in the cottage.

Warning her to stay back, he went to the door. He threw it open with a screech. The man with his back to the door could not move before Brenwyn's knife slashed into him. The final outlaw released Deira and raced into the night.

Oswiu started to run after him. When Brenwyn stopped him, he cried, "Let me go!"

"No, he is gone. He will not return."

"Damn Vikings!" the man muttered under his breath. "May Lucifer drag them all down to burn in hell!"

"They weren't Vikings," said Cyndra as she dropped to her knees by Eadburh. "They were English."

Oswiu scowled. "They wore Viking uniforms."

"Stolen from the dead," Brenwyn said, his lips as straight as his knife.

Cyndra let Brenwyn convince the farmer not to give chase while she had Gleineth get a damp rag to put on Eadburh's head. Deira sat beside her mother as she woke. She had been stunned by the blow, but there were no broken bones. When Deira began to cry in soft, broken sobs, the farm family clung to each other.

Brenwyn put his hands on Cyndra's shoulders and drew her to her feet. She flung her arms around him and let him pull her up against his strength.

"We are a good team," he whispered against her veil.

"Are we?"

He drew her back into the lean-to, shutting the door. His thumbs tipped her face back as he asked, "What is wrong, Cyndra?"

"I don't know."

He smiled tautly. "I do. You have enjoyed seeing the Norse as beasts and the English as saints. You thought all your enemies have fought beneath the black raven of the Jomsvikings. Now you see that this is not so. Some English aren't saints."

"And some Vikings aren't beasts." She curved her

hand around his nape. "It will take me some time to get used to that, I fear."

"You don't have much time to become accustomed to it. We are within a week's travel of King Swein's court."

"After you deliver your message . . ."

"You are going back to Manor Darburgh."

"And you are going to fight?"

He nodded. "If that is what my chieftain commands." When her eyes closed in pain, he brushed her lips with a swift kiss. "Nothing else has changed, milady. The conquest of England continues."

As he drew her down to the blanket, his kiss deepening as her breath grew ragged, she knew he was right again. Nothing else had changed. While she could, she wanted to be in the arms of this man who should be her most hated enemy.

Fourteen

Cyndra sat by the window in the rooms she and Brenwyn had been brought to upon their arrival at King Swein Forkbeard's castle yesterday. She yawned, wondering if she would ever be rested again.

She rose with a smile when Brenwyn entered the room. He did not return it.

"Dress in your very best, Cyndra," he ordered. "We have an audience with the king within the hour."

"We? You want me to go with you?"

His arm curved around her waist, drawing her to him. The only good thing about their journey north had been that they could be together without worrying about their past or their future. That respite of peace was over.

"No," he whispered, "I would rather you remain here, but the orders that came to me from Swein Forkbeard are for me and my traveling companions to come to his audience chamber."

"Gleineth, too?"

He nodded as the maid dipped her head and whispered a hasty prayer. "Prepare yourselves while I do the same."

"But, Brenwyn—"

He brushed her lips with a gentle kiss that could not hide the tension on his taut mouth. "The sooner this is done, the sooner we can return to Manor Darburgh." He caressed her rounded abdomen. "I want to be there before the weather grows cold and it becomes dangerous for you and our child to travel."

"I will hurry."

He smiled and turned to the door. He paused and came back, tugging her into his arms. The hunger that never could be completely sated was in his kiss. As she splayed her hands across his strong back, she tried to hide her fear. She was no more successful at concealing the truth than he was, for his eyes were dark with powerful emotions as he walked out of the room.

Cyndra pulled Gleineth to her feet as she was about to kneel in prayer. "You heard Brenwyn. We must be quick."

"I fear for you, milady. Swein Forkbeard has vowed to destroy England and all within it. I have heard that he feasts on the hearts of his enemies."

"Do not be absurd. He is a Viking like Brenwyn." Her hands clenched on her tunic as she was lifting it from its box.

"You have forgiven him for being a Viking, milady? For lying to you?"

She did not answer, because she was not sure what she would have said. Had she forgiven him? She had tried. Ignoring her despair had been simple when they traveled together, but now . . .

Cyndra quickly redressed. Opening her jewel box, she withdrew a piece at a time. Silver strands held her veil in place. The bronze pendant Brenwyn had given her fell across the front of her gown. She closed her overtunic with her best brooch.

Brenwyn returned. He had never seen Cyndra look more like the daughter of a respected ealdorman. A pinch of regret taunted him. Not once had he dared to speak the words hidden within his heart. Even a chance repetition of them could label him a traitor. He should not be sorry that Ealdorman Edgar of Manor Saeburgh was dead, but he was. He had admired Cyndra's father, who was stalwart, loyal to his inept king, and possessed a courage that had guaranteed him death. His sense of triumph at the Jomsvikings' victories had been tempered with tidings of the destruction of the manor and its residents.

He wanted to rejoice in the skill of the Jomsvikings and the defeat of the English, but Ealdorman Edgar had forced him to see that there were men of honor among the English. He despised this weakness of lamenting the death of his sworn enemy. He was a Jomsviking, who had vowed to do whatever his king asked to see England crushed.

She turned slowly. "How do I look, Brenwyn?"

His smile of approval became a scowl. He crossed the room and tore the brooch from her shoulder. He flung it to the floor and ground it under his boot.

"Brenwyn! That was my best brooch. My father—"

"Gave you a brooch with the emblem of his burgh upon it." He picked up the crumpled gold. Going to the window, he threw it to the courtyard. She put her hand on his arm, but he shook it off. "You have not given up your English ways, have you?"

"It is not easy to turn my back on all that I am."

"All you *were*."

"What I am is in part what I was." She grasped his arm, refusing to let go. "The past is part of what you are."

He shook his head. "That part of me died along with my family. You must put your English ways aside as I have done, or you may be assuring our child's death."

As he had expected, her eyes grew wide, then narrowed with understanding. "When I put the brooch on, I gave it no thought. It was my finest piece." Her breath caught, and an answering pain pricked his heart. "My father gave it to me on the first anniversary of my mother's death." Tears filled her eyes. "But I would gladly have destroyed it if I thought it would hurt you or our child."

"Cyndra—"

"No, listen to me. I will do nothing to shame you, for I love you."

He stared into her glistening eyes. "You love me?"

"Yes."

When her trembling fingers rose to brush his cheek, he kissed them. Her smile was scintillating as she drew his mouth to hers. Her gentle kiss brought forth the need for more.

She whispered, "I have wanted to tell you that for so long."

"But you didn't?"

"I was afraid you would think me a fool." She raised her chin. "But when I am within the walls of this castle, I know I cannot hide this one, special truth. My father was a warrior, and he is dead. My brother is a warrior and may be dead, too. You are a warrior, Brenwyn, and I cannot know when you may be taken from me, as well. I want you to know the truth that I love you, that it seems now that I have loved you since you comforted me after you sent the Vikings away before they could kill Sigestan and me."

His fingers edged beneath her veil, but he drew them back before they could twist in her hair. Even though he wanted to strip off her clothes and savor every bit of her in their bed, he knew they must not linger here. A gentle kiss did not ease his need, but he whispered, "We have much to talk about on our way back to Manor Darburgh, sweet one, for I love you, too."

"You love me?"

"Never doubt that, milady. Why else would I be forced to break your heart with the demands I know are so difficult for you? I wish to keep you safe and in my arms for many years to come, beloved wife."

"I am yours for always."

When Brenwyn held out his arm, Cyndra put her fingers on it. Today, she would not be required to walk behind him as a slave must. She was his wife. His *beloved* wife. With a bolstering smile for Gleineth, she walked with Brenwyn out of the room.

The castle was crowded with even more people than at Thevkil's burgh. Again and again, Cyndra looked back to be certain that Gleineth was able to follow as Brenwyn walked through the press of men. They stepped aside when they saw the badge of his rank on his shoulder.

"Geoor!" Brenwyn said with a chuckle as he paused by a set of double doors. "I am glad to see a familiar face among these strangers."

The thin man bowed his head toward Cyndra. "I hear congratulations are due to you, milady."

"Double congratulations," Brenwyn replied. "Not

only is she now my wife, but she will be giving me a child before spring arrives."

"That I had not heard." Geoor's smile appeared strained. "It seems you have garnered Freyja's blessing to conceive so quickly."

"What do you do here, my friend?"

"I have been called to attend this meeting. I understand the king is very happy with our work."

Brenwyn smiled and patted Cyndra's hand. She knew he was well pleased to see his friend acknowledged and to have someone he could trust with him when he gave his report to the king.

The doors were thrown open exactly at the time when Brenwyn Gunnarsson and Geoor Scyldsson were to appear before the king. As they were announced, pride swelled within her as she gazed at her husband. He held his sword, ready to offer to his king. His mail shone with much polishing.

She stared at luxury she had never imagined. Banners were fringed with gold. More gold ornaments were scattered about the room. She swallowed her shock as she saw that even the throne was inlaid with gold.

Swein Forkbeard, King of Jylland, was not a young man, for his heir, Canute, had helped command this successful foray. The king's hair was thin and an iron gray. His lined face told of years in the unrelenting sunshine on the north seas and in battle.

When Brenwyn halted and knelt, Cyndra did the same.

Swein called, "Under-Chieftain Brenwyn Gunnarsson, approach."

Brenwyn rose and went forward. He knelt again and placed his sword at the king's feet. "By your leave, I come on behalf of Chieftain Thevkil the Strong to report on his victories."

"Your modesty does you proud, Under-Chieftain." He looked at Geoor. "Other reports I received have told me of how deeply you were involved in these successes."

"I did as directed by my chieftain."

Swein turned to the men standing beside his throne. "Humility is something that has been missing in this court." As the men squirmed, looking uneasy, he continued, "I will have your report."

He set the packet atop his sword. One of the king's men picked it up and handed it to Swein. Not opening it, he asked, "Do you bring me these two women as a gift, Under-Chieftain?"

Cyndra hid her shock, glad when Brenwyn answered, "By your leave, this is my wife, Lady Cyndra Edgarsdottir."

"An Anglo-Saxon?" demanded a young man he knew was Canute.

"Her father was Ealdorman Edgar of Manor Saeburgh. She is my wife and the mother of my heir."

Swein called, "Come forward, woman." His eyes narrowed when she obeyed without waiting for Brenwyn to translate. He clearly had not expected that she understand his language.

She knelt by the throne.

"You are a subject of Ethelred," Swein said with a smile. "Your father was the most dangerous foe my warriors ever met. Many met their deaths on the swords of his *fyrd*. Yet now, the daughter of Ealdorman Edgar kneels to Swein of Jylland."

She forced her fear deep into her. "I am with my husband now. His ways are my ways." That was the truth, for she wished they could mingle his mixed heritage with the one she had accepted along with his promise to love her forever.

The king chuckled. "Well said, Cyndra Edgarsdottir. A brave daughter of a brave father." He drew her to stand next to him on the pedestal. "Bear witness. This lovely flower of England bows to Swein and acknowledges him as her king. So shall all of England."

A cheer filled the room as the men raised their swords and axes. The blades clanged together.

Cyndra watched with dismay. She loved Brenwyn, but at that moment was she denying her father and all she had been? She had called Brenwyn a traitor, but she was the true traitor, trading her loyalty for love.

When the shouts faded, the king smiled. "You, Cyndra Edgarsdottir, are the symbol of the future of England. This realm will accept us as her master. I would speak with you further." He glanced at his son.

Canute made a motion, and the men filed out of the room. His father spoke to him, and he called Geoor back.

Swein said, "Under-Chieftain, Canute wishes to talk to you privately. He is curious how you gained the confidence of the English thanes. If stealth can bring victory with such a small loss of life, it may prove to be a valuable tool. You are excused, Under-Chieftain, to speak with him in my private chambers."

Cyndra shot a look of desperation at Brenwyn. She could not leave until she was dismissed as well. Kneading her fingers together, she watched as Brenwyn bowed his head and walked out with Canute.

Geoor frowned as he stood beside Gleineth, who

remained on her knees. Cyndra hoped that the king did not realize that Gleineth was praying.

Swein stood and took Cyndra by the arm. Leading her to a chair by a table at the far side of the room, he sat her there. "I shall call you simply Cyndra. You will understand that the memory of your father is not a pleasant one for me."

"As you wish."

"You are a puzzle to me, Cyndra."

"A puzzle?"

Instead of answering, he motioned to Geoor. Geoor's face was tight with emotions he could not hide as Brenwyn did. The king spoke lowly to him, too fast for Cyndra to understand.

She saw Geoor's hands shake as he nodded and walked away without looking at her. She could not see where he went because Swein asked her questions so rapidly she had scarcely enough time to answer one before he fired the next at her. Most of her answers were, "I don't know, King Swein." She had no idea of the military strength of any burgh, save her father's and Manor Darburgh. If King Ethelred had ever confided his plans to her father, her father had never shared them with her.

She had thought Swein would be frustrated by her lack of information, but he only smiled when Geoor came back with a tray with two glasses on it. He took the tray and set it on the table in front of her.

"Here are two glasses of mead," he said. "Both are beautiful and promise a man pleasure." He glanced at Geoor, whose face seemed almost as lined as his king's. "One contains poison that will betray a man."

"Poison?" she gasped.

From the center of the room, Gleineth moaned. "No, not milady."

Swein ignored both of them. "A man drinks it and dies horribly. No longer is he available to do battle. In a way, he has betrayed his sword-sworn oath." He leaned toward her, no longer smiling. "Is that any different from a beautiful woman who lures one of my warriors to her bed and prevents him from being able to fulfill his duties to his king?"

"I have never asked Brenwyn to forsake his duty."

"And you never considered taking his knowledge and offering it to King Ethelred?"

"No, never!"

"Just to be sure, I thought you and I might play a game. One of these goblets contains poison. One is unadulterated. Which is which?"

He pushed the glasses closer to her, and she looked at Geoor. Was this how Brenwyn's friend had to prove his loyalty? By helping kill his friend's wife?

Swein picked up one goblet and held one out to her. His eyes gleamed as he put it to her lips.

"No!" she cried, jumping to her feet. Her chair toppled to the floor with a crash.

"Do you fear to drink, Cyndra? You do not trust your king?"

"Do you put all your subjects to such a test?"

"Drink!"

"No, milady!" cried Gleineth.

"Quiet her, Geoor Scyldsson," Swein ordered. "If her lady does not obey, slay her."

Cyndra grabbed the goblet out of his hands. She would not let him slay Gleineth, too. Slowly, she raised it to her lips. She took a sip and struggled to swallow it. She lowered the goblet to the table.

"All of it!" he snapped.

She gripped the table. A bit of the poison might not be fatal, but all of it would kill her. Closing her eyes, she took a deep breath and drained the glass. Swein had no reason to wish her dead, for she swore her allegiance to him.

With a smile, he picked up the other glass and downed the mead in one swallow. Her goblet fell from her numb fingers as Gleineth began to moan in sorrow. She clamped her hand over her mouth, wishing she could be ill and expel the poison from her. Swein would not allow that.

She swayed as her knees folded. "Please, give me an antidote. Don't kill the child."

He caught her chin in his hand as she fell to her knees. "I return you to the arms of your father. Remind him how he killed my best friend and how I vowed to see him repaid. Let his last drop of blood die with you."

"Tell Brenwyn," she gasped, looking past him to Geoor, "tell him that I love him."

Swein cursed and shoved her to the floor. She wanted to push herself up, but she could not move. The darkness sucked her down into it. There was no escape.

Brenwyn entered the throne room and dropped to his knees, waiting for his king to note his arrival. When he heard no voices, he wanted to raise his head to see how Cyndra fared. He knew Swein wished to quiz her as his son had quizzed Brenwyn. His answers had seemed to satisfy the king's heir. Cyndra's should satisfy the king, too, but he knew how difficult it was for her to be among her father's enemies. He was grateful Geoor and Gleineth had remained here with her.

"Rise, Under-Chieftain Brenwyn Gunnarsson."

He obeyed. The rest of the room was empty. Where was Cyndra? Had she left with Geoor and Gleineth? He clasped his hands behind him, glad that she had his friend to watch over her.

"I have completed my discussion with your Cyndra, Under-Chieftain," the king said without emotion. "Her version of your meeting and love affair is interesting."

"I am certain she was quite willing to answer any questions you might have had."

Swein bent and, from where it had rolled under the table, picked up a goblet. "She did once I put her to the test." He held up two empty drinking vessels.

Brenwyn's stomach twisted. He began to speak several times, but the words would not pass the clog in his throat. He could not express his rage to his king. "She gave you the answers you required?" he finally asked.

"She gave me answers."

"It was not necessary to frighten her so. She is a woman. She has nothing of military importance to hide." His hands opened and closed as he fought not to grasp his sword and demand a few answers of his own.

"Nothing? The daughter of Ealdorman Edgar, who took too many of my men into death with him? That Lady Cyndra has denied her father I cannot believe," stated Swein icily. "Is it the truth or did she attach herself to you in hopes of revenging her family?"

"When Lady Cyndra agreed to be my wife and

accept our ways, she had no knowledge of her father's death and the destruction of Manor Saeburgh."

Brenwyn saw Swein was surprised by this information. *Where is Cyndra?* He wanted to shout that question. Every second that passed knotted his gut more painfully. "Did you have the antidote given to Cyndra?"

Swein glanced at the goblet in his hand before setting it on the table. He poured more wine into another glass and walked to his throne and sat. He took a leisurely sip of wine. "There are others who will give you a son, Brenwyn Gunnarsson. I know Chieftain Yngvi Hnaefsson has a daughter who would make a good wife for you." He smiled. "Yes, Thyre Yngvisdottir would make an excellent wife for you, Under-Chieftain, for you would be allying your line with one nearly as highly placed as your king's. You have served me well and deserve this reward."

"I must remind you, sire, that I have a wife."

"Do you?"

His jaw tightened as he thought of the poison used and its effects on its victim. He gripped the hilt of his sword, then released it. Everything he was, everything he had vowed to be, everything he had vowed to do stayed his hand.

"Surely the daughter of my truest friend and a fine home in Jylland sounds better than remaining on this blighted isle for the rest of your life," Swein said.

"I would be pleased to return to Jylland, but it is with my wife and our child I would choose to travel."

Swein rose and slammed his goblet on the table. "Why can't you understand what your friend did?"

"Friend?"

"Geoor Scyldsson prepared the poison for her. He knows how to obey an order. Do you?"

"I obey, my king." He could barely speak past his clenched teeth.

"I will not have my plans for England risked because of your lust for this woman. Do you understand, Under-Chieftain Brenwyn Gunnarsson?"

He hesitated. Was this why Thevkil had tried to keep Cyndra at his burgh? No, Thevkil would have slain her, too, as soon as Brenwyn left. "I understand." He must understand, for it was his death-vow that he had sworn his allegiance upon.

"Prepare to leave. My ship sails for Jylland on the evening tide. You will accompany me there to inform my chieftains of what you have learned that will help them win this island before the next warm season passes."

Brenwyn nodded, then asked, "Does she live?"

"What was once is no longer." Raising his goblet, he added, "You are dismissed."

Brenwyn bowed his head and walked to the door. His stride was smooth, but his heart lurched with pain. Somehow, he found his way to the rooms they had shared. Only when he threw open the cupboard where Cyndra's things had hung and saw that it was empty, did he realize that Swein intended to obliterate all signs of her.

"Cyndra!" he shouted, as if his voice could reach her. He sank to his knees by the bed they had shared last night and whispered, "I love you. Forgive me."

The sobs that ripped from him were of a man who had not cried in more years than he could remember. Pulling his knife, he drew back his left sleeve. He slashed it across his left forearm.

"Cyndra, I shall die in battle, bathed in honor and

with the blood of my enemies." His voice broke as he repeated her words.

He would accept the first deadly mission he could. As he fulfilled both his death-vows, his blood would be spilled in the service of the man who had murdered his wife. Then his heart would stop beating with the rhythm of Cyndra's name and he would find her once more in death.

Where they would be parted no more.

Fifteen

The hut leaned away from the wind blowing off
the northern sea. Mud covered the stones and
branches heaped together. A piece of tattered material served as a doorway. No windows broke the
curved walls. There could be no fire inside, for the
roof was smooth with dirt.

A stone was set by the door. On it, Gleineth sat,
grinding meal for tomorrow's bread. Today's bread
was baking in the coals of the fire in the sand. All
the bread was unleavened, for there was no money
to buy yeast from the brewer.

When she heard a sound from within the hut, she
looked over her shoulder. She smiled as the shadows
moved and took form.

"Good morning, Cyndra."

Cyndra rubbed her eyes as she stepped out into
the sunshine. She drew a ripped cloth over the baby
in her arms. Even though her clothes were frayed,
she wore them with pride. Her underdress was shiny
where the wool had worn thin, and her veil barely
covered her head.

She sat and, loosening her tunic, put the baby to
her breast and leaned back. Only at moments like
this, when she had a rare moment to sit still, did

she think of anything but the struggle to survive on this strand.

The baby had her blond hair, but had inherited his father's sea-blue eyes. This child should never have been born. Geoor had warned her to make sure the baby did not survive, for she would not have a second chance to escape the king's wrath.

Geoor . . . although she had told herself that he had had no choice, for Swein would have ordered him dead, too, she could not forgive him.

He *had* saved her life by mixing enough of the poison to make her senseless, but not kill her. It had acted like a sleeping potion, so she had seemed dead as he took her out of the castle to dispose of her. Deep in the forest along the shore, he had left her to Gleineth's care.

His parting words still stung like a fresh blow. "The king has accepted Brenwyn's offer to trade his life for yours, milady. You must never return to the castle or speak of this to anyone. Disappear. Find yourself a new husband and build a new family." He had put his hand on her stomach. "If this one is born alive, slay it. Swein will not allow any child of yours and Brenwyn's blood to live."

"No," she had moaned. "You must help me stop Brenwyn. He must not give his life for me."

"Too late, milady. His life is Swein's. Do not come seeking his final resting place and tempt Swein's mercy." He had left her there with only a bag of her clothes and Gleineth.

For food, they had sold the clothes and all her jewelry except the pendant with Thor's hammer. That would betray them to the English, so she still wore it close to her skin, keeping it safe. Gleineth's one attempt to sneak into the castle had garnered her no information other than that Brenwyn Gunnarsson was gone, and no one knew if he lived or was dead.

In the months since, they had found a home in this hovel and switched roles to protect the unborn child. Gleineth pretended to be a ceorl and Cyndra her slave. When the baby had come right on time, he was baptized by the priest in a nearby village with his grandfather's name. Only Cyndra added his father's name to it.

"Gleineth!" came a shout from the trees behind the hovel.

Jumping to her feet, Gleineth smiled even more broadly. She ran to be enfolded into the arms of the smith whose forge was a short distance away.

Cyndra looked down at her son. She was happy for Gleineth. Aldfrith was a kind man with no ambitions beyond his work. Her maid need not worry about her happiness being stolen by vows or swordsworn oaths that led only to death.

As Edgar greedily sucked, she placed her fingers against his dough-soft cheek. Her eyes filled with tears that came too readily. At first, she had thought it was only the melancholy that affected women after childbirth; but as time went on, she knew it was far more than that. While she had been pregnant, she had not thought past her child's birth. Now she could see the hopelessness of her future.

How proud Brenwyn would be to see his fine son! Edgar Brenwynsson already showed signs of his father's stubborn determination.

"Edgar," she whispered, "your mother is a foolish woman. I know your father is watching over us, but I wish he were here."

As she wiped away the tear that had dripped onto

his ragged blanket, she heard Gleineth's joyous voice. She knew Gleineth was happy here as she had not been since they left Manor Saeburgh.

Manor Saeburgh. The very name sent pain through her. She could not return to her father's burgh. It no longer existed. She could not find a welcome among the invaders, for Geoor's prophecy of death for her and Edgar would come true.

"Cyndra! Grand tidings!"

Cyndra managed to smile as Gleineth rushed over to her, dragging Aldfrith in her wake. Aldfrith was almost as thin as Geoor Scyldsson, belying his ready strength when he stood beside his forge and forced iron to acknowledge him as its master.

"What is it?" she asked. "Good day to you, Aldfrith."

"The same to you, Cyndra." He squatted beside her. "I see young Edgar still thinks he is a piglet."

She laughed. The smith had a way of being able to tease her into putting her grief aside. When he glanced at Gleineth, she guessed she had her maid to thank for his efforts. "Edgar is growing so fast that he has no time for anything else but eating and occasionally sleeping."

"If only he would learn to sleep at night . . ." Gleineth rolled her eyes and chuckled.

"What are these grand tidings?" Cyndra suspected she already knew when Aldfrith took Gleineth's hand.

Gleineth said, "Aldfrith has asked me to marry him."

"Blessings on both of you and every happiness." She reached out to hug Gleineth, then, when the baby protested, sat back. "I shall have to congratulate you later."

"Then it pleases you?"

"Of course." She glanced at Aldfrith, whose smile became a puzzled frown. She had become so accustomed to the equality in the house on the shore that she had forgotten that Gleineth needed her permission to wed. Sharp laughter threatened to burst forth. What could be more ludicrous than an ealdorman's ragged daughter giving permission to her equally ragged ceorl to marry under these conditions? Remembering her role, she bowed her head. "What makes you happy makes me happy, Gleineth."

"You and Edgar will be welcome in our home." Her maid's eyes did not shift, and Cyndra realized Gleineth was struggling, in the midst of her joy, to protect her.

"I thank you." Her smile became more sincere. "You have many to share these glad tidings with. I shall watch the baking bread while you do that."

Cyndra leaned back against the mud wall as Gleineth and Aldfrith, hand-in-hand, walked along the strand toward the path leading to the village. She closed her eyes as she shifted Edgar to her other breast. For a moment, she need not pretend.

Yes, she was happy for Gleineth. How many times had her maid flirted and fallen in and out of love as quickly as the coming and going of a rainbow? They had been here more than a half year, and once she had met Aldfrith, she had had no interest in any other man.

The smell of burning bread tore Cyndra out of her thoughts. Pulling the bread from the fire, she dropped it on a piece of wood and shook her fingers. She stuck one that threatened to blister into her mouth.

Her eyes widened as she saw a familiar silhouette

walking toward her. His youthful stride was easy as he swung a basket in each hand. The wind blew back his hair from his shoulders that still had not attained a man's breadth, and the sunlight glinted off the knife at his waist.

Sigestan!

She was running along the shore before her mind had completely formed his name. Was it possible? Was her brother alive?

Cyndra stopped in midstep as the lad dropped to sweep the basket through the water to catch fish. His hair was as ebony as the forest at night.

He looked up at her. "What do you want?" he growled.

"Nothing."

"Then be off with you. I don't have enough to share with beggars."

She backed away, pulling the cloth more tightly around Edgar. He snarled a curse as she turned and hurried toward the hut. At her or at the sea which had not put a feast into his basket?

No matter. Cyndra knew she could no longer ignore the duty she had put off through the winter. Both Thevkil and Swein had bragged about the death of her father. Not once had they mentioned her brother. If they had been certain of his death, they would have taunted her with that as well.

Sigestan must still be alive and in hiding as she was. Mayhap he had spent the winter raising a *fyrd* to bring insurrection against the Vikings. *Never be defeated. Not even in defeat.* Father had taught that lesson to Sigestan as he had to her. The echo of the battle cry of Manor Saeburgh rang through her head, and she looked toward the west.

She smiled. She knew, at last, what she should do.

* * *

"You cannot go, milady!"

Cyndra glanced up, startled at the title Gleineth had not spoken to her in months. "Take care, Gleineth."

"Advice you should take for yourself. Why are you leaving? You have a home here with Aldfrith and me."

"I appreciate your offer." She turned on her knees, for they could not stand inside the hut, and took Gleineth's hands. "You have served me well, following me when I knew you did not agree with my choices."

"I did not agree with them, but now I understand them." She sat back on her heels. "For Aldfrith, I would do as you did for the man you loved."

Cyndra closed her eyes. One thing had not changed. It would never change. To speak Brenwyn's name chanced death from both the English and the Jomsvikings. It now could be heard only in her heart and her whispers to Edgar when the rest of the world slept.

"And now," she said softly, "you must understand that I have to find out if Sigestan is alive."

"Let him find you!"

"Why would he look here?"

"He shares the blood of your father, milady. He will not rest until he finds you."

"Nor can I until I find him." She closed the small bag that held the rags that she used to diaper the baby. It was all she had to carry with her. "At least, I know a place to begin seeking him."

"Manor Saeburgh is destroyed. The Vikings will

be certain no one settles there, especially your brother."

"I'm not going to Manor Saeburgh."

Gleineth grasped her sleeve. "No, milady! You can't return to Manor Darburgh."

"It is where Sigestan would have gone first. From there, I may be able to follow and find him."

"The Jomsvikings there will see you dead."

She shook her head. "You have heard the reports. The Jomsvikings may not be within Manor Darburgh. They have been called south by their chieftains to join the battle against King Ethelred."

"Those may be only rumors."

"They may be." She touched the hidden amulet that would mean their deaths if any Englishman saw it. "We have many allies within the walls of Manor Darburgh. Someone will help us."

Gleineth whispered a prayer, then said, "Very well, milady. When do we leave?"

"We? You need not come. Your life is here now."

"My life is yours, milady. I serve you."

She could not speak, overwhelmed by Gleineth's loyalty. Taking her maid's hand, she blinked back tears when Gleineth raised it to her forehead in a pose of servitude that was older than legend. She wanted to fling her arms around Gleineth and hug her as she had tried this morning at the betrothal announcement. She could not. The easy camaraderie of the past months was gone. Once more, she was Lady Cyndra, daughter of Ealdorman Edgar and widow of Under-Chieftain Brenwyn Gunnarsson.

"We leave with dawn," she whispered. "Edgar usually wakes just before sunrise, so I shall feed him before we set out on our way."

"As you wish, milady."

"You must speak with Aldfrith of this."

Gleineth gave her a thankful smile. "I shall go now, milady, if I may."

She nodded. As Gleineth rushed out the door, she doubted if her maid would return before dawn. This one night with her betrothed might be the only one she had, because their journey would be long and could lead only to death.

When she stepped out of the hut in the first gray of dawn, Cyndra was not surprised to see Aldfrith standing beside Gleineth. She was shocked when he came forward and dropped to his knees. What had Gleineth told him? The truth? All of it?

"Milady," he said in a serious tone so unlike his usual jovial voice, "Gleineth has shared with me the tale of your trials and your search for your brother and your hopes of finding him before the accursed Norse slay him. I am not a swordsman, but allow me to accompany you on your journey."

"I don't know when we'll return here."

"I understand that." He looked up at Gleineth. "When you leave, there is nothing to keep me here, for I fled my home before the Vikings as you did."

Cyndra hid her amazement. She had not guessed Aldfrith was a newcomer to the settlement in the trees, too. "If you wish to join us, you are welcome."

"As my husband," Gleineth said with a shy smile.

"You married?"

"Last night, milady."

She smiled. "Then there is no further reason to delay, is there?"

Aldfrith stood and hefted a pack that clanked. It must contain some of his tools. Her smile grew wider. With his skills, they could trade for food and information on their way.

Mayhap, just mayhap, she might be able to find Sigestan and build a new life for herself with the family she had left. It would be a dream come true . . . but one without Brenwyn. She had to put that dream aside.

Forever.

Sixteen

Cyndra waved aside the smoke from the fire of Aldfrith's makeshift forge. She had thought she would grow accustomed to it after two fortnights of traveling west, stopping at each crossroads to trade his skills for enough food to reach the next crossroads.

Turning her back on the smoke, she drew Edgar from her breast and hooked her dress closed. She smiled down at the baby, whose lips still were pursed. Just yesterday, he had started making silly sounds that soon would become words. She had to watch him more closely because he crawled on his belly through the grass and sometimes pushed himself up on all fours, although he had not yet figured out how to move on hands and knees. Her fears that the poison she had swallowed would damage him had been for naught. He was growing so quickly and was happiest when he was gnawing on a carrot to bring his teeth out.

Cyndra looked up as she heard running steps. Children should not be playing so close to the forge. They could fall and get hurt.

She came to her feet as Gleineth and another woman burst out of the smoke. Hild! The woman had been the most troublesome ceorl in Manor Darburgh's kitchens. Were they so close to the burgh?

"Milady," cried Hild, dropping to her knees and pressing her face to Cyndra's feet, "you must leave at once."

"Leave?"

Hild raised her head. "Is it true? Is Brenwyn Gunnarsson dead?"

"Brenwyn Gunnarsson?" asked Aldfrith, stepping away from his forge and wiping his face with his leather apron. "That is a Norse name. Does he hold Manor Darburgh?"

"No longer." Hild hid her face in Cyndra's dress again. "You must leave, milady. Thane Morcar has retaken the manor in the past week."

"Morcar?" she whispered. "He is dead!"

"I pray it were so, but he is alive. He used some sort of treachery to take the burgh. I know not what, but he has allies well in favor with the king and Edmund Ironside. Thane Morcar is riding with his *fyrd* now to secure the lands that are his again. Milady, you must go!"

Fright like she had never known made Cyndra back away as if Hild ailed with some deadly disease. She had not been this terrified when she drank from the poisoned goblet in King Swein's audience room. Then her fate was death. Morcar would be sure she suffered worse for falling in love with Brenwyn. She looked at her child. If he learned of Edgar . . .

When Gleineth took her arm to keep her from stepping on the coals, Cyndra whispered, "Thevkil told me he was dead."

"Thevkil?" gasped Aldfrith. "How did you come to speak to him?" Fury darkened his normally tranquil eyes.

"Not now," she said, desperately. "I will explain later. Now we have to hide." She glanced at Hild. "Thank you."

"You allowed Brenwyn to promote my man when Morcar had refused him that promotion."

"Brenwyn promoted? A Viking?" Aldfrith's scowl was as dark as the smoke stains on his face. "What is all this?"

Gleineth cried, "Heed milady. We must go."

"But—"

"I will explain," Cyndra said, her voice again calm, for she could not panic, "if you do not value your life. The man whom my father betrothed me to has retaken Manor Darburgh. If he finds you with me, you are dead, Aldfrith. He will not wait for explanations. He will slay you simply because you helped me."

"Heed her," Gleineth urged again.

"Go!" cried Hild. "I will see the fire put out. You cannot linger."

Cyndra was not sure which of their words, or if it had been all of them together, persuaded the smith. He grabbed his tools and stuffed them into his sack. Putting his arm around Gleineth, he herded her along the road back in the direction they had traveled. Cyndra smiled at Hild, then followed. She wondered if there were any place she and Edgar could be safe.

When the woods grew thick, Aldfrith led the way through the trees. He paused near a thicket. Cyndra sank to the ground. Edgar wiggled, so she put him down and watched he did not crawl away.

Aldfrith sat beside her. "The truth."

"Milady," added Gleineth, kneeling beside him and putting her hand on his arm.

He frowned at her, then nodded. "The truth, if you will, milady."

"I am Lady Cyndra, the daughter of Ealdorman Edgar of Manor Saeburgh."

"Ealdorman?" he gasped. "That is the highest rank in England, except for the king."

"And I was betrothed to Thane Morcar of Manor Darburgh."

"Morcar? Is he Edgar's father? You said his father was dead."

"I thought Morcar was dead."

He scowled. "Yes, you said that. That Thevkil told you that. Thevkil the Strong?"

"Yes." She plucked a piece of grass from the youngster's mouth.

"How did you come to speak to that Viking chieftain?"

"I spoke with him when I went with Edgar's father to his court." She took a deep breath as Gleineth patted her hand. "Edgar's father's name was Under-Chieftain Brenwyn Gunnarsson. He was a Jomsviking and captured Manor Darburgh. Part of his prize was me."

His frown faded into pity. "Forgive me, milady. I should have known that you do not speak of this to protect Gleineth, who suffered through this horror with you."

"You don't understand, Aldfrith!" She watched his features grow rigid as she whispered, "I loved Brenwyn from the moment I met him while he garnered information to give to Thevkil. I loved him, Aldfrith. I love him still. When Swein Forkbeard was set to kill me, Brenwyn gave his life so Edgar and I could live."

His eyes widened in abhorrence.

She picked up the baby and rose. "Do not stare at me like that," she begged.

"You became a Viking's mistress of your own free will?"

"I became his wife."

"Of your own free will?"

She started to reply, but a voice shouted her name. Morcar! Someone must have tipped him off before Hild was able to warn her. If she let him find them, he would force her to watch as he killed her friends and her son. Mayhap he had not guessed who traveled with her.

Turning to Gleineth, she shoved Edgar into her maid's arms. "Take my son. Go to Manor Tiwburgh. It is about a league north of here."

"To Geoor Scyldsson?" she choked.

She nodded. "Tell him that Edgar is the son of Under-Chieftain Brenwyn Gunnarsson and Cyndra Edgarsdottir and ask for sanctuary for my baby."

"But he told you to kill this child."

"Brenwyn is dead, and I soon shall be. No one needs to know that Edgar is our child." Tears blurred her son's face as she looked at him for what she feared was the last time. "Please, Gleineth." From under her dress, she pulled the amulet. She slipped it over Edgar's head. "If he wishes to know, tell him that Morcar has me and I would be grateful for his aid."

"Milady, how can I leave—"

She looked past Gleineth to Aldfrith. "Get them to Geoor. He is your only hope of not being killed." Her voice broke. "Don't let Morcar kill Edgar."

Aldfrith glanced over his shoulder at the sounds of many men pushing through the underbrush. "To save Gleineth, I will do as you request."

"Save my son. Please."

Without another word, he took the baby from Gleineth and pushed her ahead of him away from the road and the approaching men.

Closing her eyes, Cyndra took a deep breath. She heard her name shouted. Checking that the others had vanished, she called, "I am here, Morcar."

The bushes were shoved aside. With her chin high, she met Morcar's triumphant gaze. It took all her strength not to race after Gleineth and Aldfrith.

"So, my wayward betrothed has returned to Manor Darburgh." He eyed her up and down. "You look no better than a beggar."

She did not let his words hurt her. He would use more than words to punish her for loving Brenwyn. "I must admit it is a surprise that you are here. I thought you too cowardly to attack the Jomsvikings."

"I have won back my manor from your lover, Cyndra. Did he abandon you when he tired of you?"

"He is dead."

He smiled with satisfaction. "That is too bad. I would have liked the opportunity to kill him myself."

"It seems you are denied that."

His smile wavered as he snarled, "So, you come crawling back to beg my forgiveness. Where is Brenwyn's bastard?"

"There is no child."

He struck her face harshly. At her soft cry of pain, he shoved her against a tree and gripped her cheeks in his hand. "Where is the child, Cyndra, and your new lover? I never guessed Ealdorman Edgar's daughter would be such a whore."

"If you speak of the child I carried along the road,

it is not mine. I was traveling with its family. Where they have gone, I do not know. When they heard you, they fled."

Morcar laughed. "Fine protectors you find for yourself!"

"I had to depend on whom I could after Brenwyn gave his life for mine."

"Always the noble hero, was he? I thought he would tire of your lack of fire and leave you. Or does he have as poor a choice in mistresses as in allegiances?"

"I was not his mistress. I was his wife."

"Wife? You married that Norse dog?" He scowled. "What happened to him?"

"He is dead by Swein's order."

"Did he die because he finally showed that he is a coward?"

She blinked back tears. "He died because he loved me."

"Then he is as great a fool as I had thought." He eyed her up and down. "Are you telling the truth, or is this another of your lies?"

"I have no reason to lie. Until this hour, I had no idea that you were alive, for I had been told you were dead. When I learned the truth, I thought I should continue on to Manor Saeburgh, knowing you would not want me."

"You were wrong." He jerked her into his arms.

His mouth ground into hers, and she fought not to pull away. The longer she could distract him, the greater the chance was that Gleineth could lead Aldfrith and the baby to Geoor's burgh.

"You would find no welcome at Manor Saeburgh," he growled. "It is gone, along with everyone there."

"Save for me," came a voice she had thought

never to hear again. It was deeper, but it was no less beloved.

She pushed away from Morcar and stared at another face she had feared she would never see again. "Sigestan!"

He was taller by almost a head, and his shoulders had taken on a breadth that would rival Brenwyn's. On his face and his bare forearms were scars she had never seen, and she knew he was gaining vengeance for their father's death with his sword arm.

Just as Brenwyn had.

Lurching forward, she put her hands on his arms. Then she hugged him. He held her so tightly she could not breathe before he pushed her back a half-step. When he looked down, she saw damp spots on his tunic where her breasts had brushed him. If Morcar saw and guessed she was nursing Brenwyn's child, his rage would be more than any she had seen.

Sigestan pulled off his cloak and threw it over her shoulders. "Cyndra, let us get you back to Manor Darburgh where you can clean yourself and find clothes more befitting an ealdorman's daughter."

"Yes," she whispered, wanting to thank him, but knowing she could not now.

Morcar seized her arm. "I am the thane here. I say—"

"We are upon your lands, Morcar," Sigestan said with a dignity she had never heard in his voice, "but I need not remind you that I am, with my father's death, an ealdorman." Drawing Cyndra's arm out of Morcar's grip, he put his arm around her shoulders and steered her toward the road.

She did not look back.

* * *

As she entered the gates of Manor Darburgh, Cyndra was not sure whether to cheer or sob. Morcar had not sent men to chase after Gleineth and the baby. He was too furious that she had wed Brenwyn to think of anything else.

She held Sigestan's cloak close to her as she looked around the burgh. The buildings had not changed, but she saw bloodstains on the walls. Charred thatch topped the stable. This time, the battle to take Manor Darburgh had been far more violent. Looking up at the guard posts on the wall, she gasped when she saw Cerdic there. The situation might not be so hopeless if she could persuade him and her brother to be her allies.

But would they when she had married a man they were sworn to hate?

When she looked at her brother, he shook his head. She sighed. So much she wanted to ask, but he was right. She must wait until they were alone.

"My sister will join you for the evening meal," Sigestan said with that same imperious tone that Father had used with a recalcitrant ceorl.

Morcar grumbled, then strode away. She guessed he did not argue because he wished to keep Ealdorman Sigestan as his ally.

Ealdorman Sigestan. That sounded so peculiar, for she had not thought he would have that title for many years to come. Grief threatened to undo her.

Calling for someone to bring Cyndra some unripped clothes, Sigestan led her to the bur that had been hers. He opened the door, and she saw it was just as she had left it when she rode with Brenwyn to go to Thevkil's court. That had been so long ago, seemingly more than a lifetime ago.

Edgar's lifetime.

"Why did you come back here?" Sigestan asked, leaving the door open and pushing aside the shutters on the window. She knew he wanted to be certain no one was able to sneak close to listen.

"I thought I might find a haven here and information about you." She sat on the bench and sighed. "Thevkil told me that Morcar was dead."

"And you believed a Viking?"

"He had no reason to lie to me . . . then." She waited until he sat on the hearth stones, then said, "Tell me why *you* are here."

"When it was clear that Manor Saeburgh was lost, Father ordered me and two ceorls to gather the surviving women and children. We took them to the convent, where we stood our ground against the attack. It was not a fierce one, for the Norse contented themselves with destroying every stick of Manor Saeburgh."

When she winced, he put his hand on her shoulder. She put hers over it.

"I came to Manor Darburgh," he went on, "for the same reason you did. Hoping to find you. When I discovered the burgh was held by a handful of Jomsvikings, I gathered men to take it, thinking you might be within as a prisoner. Morcar heard of my efforts and brought his surviving men with him to help." He drew up one knee and rested his elbow on it, looking for a moment like the youngster she remembered. "It was then that I heard how Morcar left his men to be slaughtered while he and his thanes ran from the Jomsvikings."

"That is no surprise. He is a coward." She frowned. "But I saw Cerdic on the wall. He is no coward."

"No. From what he tells me, Morcar sent him and the few surviving men of the manor's *fyrd* on a useless mission to find him some wine to celebrate the victory he expected would be his. By the time Cerdic heard of the debacle, he returned to be met by Morcar fleeing the field."

She closed her eyes and sighed. Without a strong leader, the *fyrd* had been doomed.

"I learned as well," Sigestan continued in a strained voice, "that Brenwyn was a traitor."

She shook her head. "No, not a traitor. He was always a Jomsviking. That is why the ones attacking Manor Saeburgh the day before Father sent me here left at his orders."

"Tell me I heard wrong, sister. You did not marry him, did you?"

"Yes, I married him, because he won my heart."

"And you bore him a child?"

She stood and went to the bed she had shared with Brenwyn in those special hours she ached to know again. Picking up the small statues of Frey and Freyja which Geoor had given them, she smiled. The Norse gods had blessed them with a son Brenwyn had never seen and she might never see again.

"Edgar Brenwynsson is with Gleineth, who escaped without Morcar seeing her."

Sigestan surged to his feet. "You used Father's name for a Viking—"

"For *my* son." She caught his hands. "Sigestan, Edgar is your nephew, the only other of Father's blood to survive."

He closed his eyes, then held out his arms. Again, she hugged him as she had when he was so much younger. "Where is he?" he whispered.

"Gleineth is taking him to Manor Tiwburgh."

He pushed her back. "That is held by a Joms-viking—"

"Named Geoor Scyldsson. He is Brenwyn's friend and saved me from death, Sigestan. I hope he will do the same for Edgar."

"I shall find a way to find out."

"You can't bring Edgar here. Morcar will have him killed."

"As he will you, if he discovers this." He scowled as he dabbed at the drying spots on his tunic. "If he beds you, he will learn the truth."

"Then I can't let him bed me." She shuddered. The very idea sickened her. She looked down at the statues she held and smiled. "He will not bed me if he thinks I have taken a vow to the church."

"The Norse church?"

She chuckled. "No, I will tell him I have become a nun. Do you think he will believe me?"

Sigestan shrugged. "He is more than a little insane. I was planning to leave by week's end, for he seemed to have no idea where you were. This lie may be your only protection until we can find a way to sneak you out of here and get Edgar and return to our father's lands."

At a knock on the door, he went and returned with a neatly folded tunic and underdress. She took them, putting them on the bed. Reaching for the pin on her tunic, she paused. She must not change. She wished she could wear something other than these filthy tatters, but she needed to look as if she had given up all worldly goods.

She prayed this deception would work. Otherwise, she would spend this night in Morcar's bed.

* * *

Morcar frowned when Cyndra entered the great hall. From the high table, he shouted, "Lady Cyndra, go and dress as is appropriate for your rank."

All conversation halted as every eye focused on her. She dipped in a curtsy. "I cannot do as you request, milord. I have accepted orders from a source higher than yours."

"What nonsense is this? Do as I told you!"

Without raising her eyes, she said, "I cannot. I thought you were dead, Morcar. When Brenwyn was killed, I needed aid to set my life to rights once more. I went to the abbey at Ely and requested sanctuary. There I found a peace that healed my heart." Her face came up to reveal an inner glow, an expression she had practiced with Sigestan. "I took my vows as a nun, Morcar."

"You, a nun?" He laughed. "What a waste of womanhood!"

"I must return to Ely to be released from my obligations. Only then can I return to be your wife."

He leaped down from the platform and grasped her arms. "You are going nowhere. Your vows of chastity will be broken this night when you welcome me to your bed."

"No."

Again he laughed. "It is not your choice, Cyndra." He pulled her to him and kissed her hard.

Sigestan began, "Morcar—"

Athelbert growled a curse and ripped her away from Morcar. Fear shone in his eyes. Cyndra had not suspected Morcar's favored thane was terrified of heaven's wrath.

"Milord," he cried, "do you wish to risk all you have gained? Surely you have seen you have God's favor. Do you want to lose that? A messenger can get to Ely and back in a month. You must wait, mi-lord. You must!"

A murmur of assent grew into a wave around the room. Morcar scowled at her. Mumbling with rage, he stormed out of the hall.

She straightened her clothes. "Thank you, Athelbert."

"You stupid woman!" he snarled. "See if you are grateful when Morcar takes you after being denied for two fortnights."

"If you feel that way—"

"Do you honestly think I want to help you? Your punishment will be that much more severe for forcing him to wait to bed you. Do you think he has forgiven you for giving yourself to that traitorous Viking? Mayhap God will. Mayhap the devil will, but not Morcar! I will convince Morcar to let me watch. What fun!"

Sigestan intruded to say, "Athelbert, you are excused."

"Mayhap I am, but can you excuse your sister's actions?"

"She often spoke of hearing a higher call," he said with dignity, as if he truly misunderstood Athelbert's comment. "Like our mother, she has long done good works for the sisters in the convent not far from Manor Saeburgh." When Athelbert started to snap another insult, Sigestan repeated, "You are excused."

As Sigestan held out his hand and she put hers on it, he led her to the raised table for their meal. She tried to hide her shiver of fear. Her brother was right. Morcar was more than a little mad, and his followers were just as insane. She wondered if any of them would survive long enough to escape from Manor Darburgh.

Seventeen

Cyndra glanced up from the small shirt she was embroidering for Edgar. If someone had noticed what she was doing, she would claim she was making clothes for the needy. It helped pass the time to do something for her son, who was too far away.

Sigestan had not been able to devise an excuse to go to Manor Tiwburgh. Morcar watched him as closely as he did Cyndra, seeking proof that they were lying. The month of her reprieve was nearly gone, and she had not heard if Edgar were alive or dead.

Her needle remained poised halfway to the next stitch as she heard the gates being swung closed. She rushed to the door of her bur. The *fyrd* was gathering their weapons as orders were shouted from every direction. One voice carried over the others with a calm authority.

Cerdic! She was glad he was here to sort order out of the chaos. But, mayhap, it would have been better if he were not here. Now the *fyrd* had a strong leader who had learned well from Brenwyn.

She put her needlework on the bench as Hild hurried to the bur. Hild had appointed herself as Cyndra's body-servant, clearly trying to atone for giving her warning too late.

Breathlessly, Hild said, "Thane Morcar requests your presence in the great hall, milady."

"I will be there as soon as I can." She turned to the shield on the wall and checked her hair. On one thing, Morcar had insisted upon, and she had been glad to relent. Her clothes were now without holes and rips.

"You should not risk angering him now."

She laughed. "I believe he has other things to concern him than me. It seems Morcar's neighbors have come calling. This will be an interesting visit for all of us, especially the thane of Manor Darburgh."

Hild grinned wickedly. Cyndra knew she was eager to see Morcar gone because he had demoted her husband, stealing Hild's rank as well.

When Cyndra walked into the great hall, her brother stepped forward to offer his arm. He did not look at her, but said softly, "It begins, Cyndra."

"At last."

"But where shall it end for you?"

She looked at him and away before Morcar took note. Trust Sigestan to see the very core of her dilemma. She hated the Jomsvikings, but she loved Brenwyn. Did his death cut all her ties to the invaders? What of her son, whose blood was partly Norse? She could not deny what he was without denying his father.

When Morcar motioned from his chair at the high table for Cyndra to join him, she was glad to put these uncomfortable thoughts from her mind. Sigestan stood behind her, his hand on her shoulder. She guessed his other one was on the hilt of his sword.

Morcar growled something she could not understand.

Rather than ask him to repeat himself, she asked, "Why have you gathered us here like this?"

He swore. "You know, Cyndra. Your lover's compatriots are ready to demand my surrender."

"My husband's," she corrected without lowering her voice. She saw the glances exchanged throughout the hall. The ceorls had been privy to her plans to marry Brenwyn, but they had known better than to mention those plans to Morcar. By her acknowledging it so publicly, she saved them from being punished for speaking of it.

Morcar cursed again, then said, "I shall listen to their demands and then throw their corpses into the dung heap where they belong."

Horns sounded. She prayed his pageantry would not end in bloodshed. When two men entered the hall, Cyndra bit her lip. Geoor and his companion walked toward them as if they were welcome guests.

"Morcar of Manor Darburgh, I am Geoor Scyldsson, here on the command of my chieftain to request that you cede this manor to King Canute Sweinsson."

"King Canute?" Cyndra gasped. Her brother tightened his grip on her shoulder, warning her to silence. She had not heard that Swein Forkbeard was dead.

Morcar ignored her. "This is English land, ruled by an English thane. You will take this burgh only upon the deaths of myself and my *fyrd*."

"My men outnumber yours by more than three to one. They await my chieftain's orders just beyond your walls. Do you want to see your manor destroyed and your women and children killed?"

"We are English. We do not surrender to Norse dogs."

Geoor nodded, no emotion on his face. "Then I must inform you that at sunrise, my chieftain will order his men to lay siege to your manor, Thane Morcar. If any of your people desire sanctuary, I welcome them and promise them safety." He looked at Cyndra.

She met his gaze calmly, even though a dozen questions in her heart demanded answers. Seeing his sympathy, she wanted to tell him she was fine, that she had forgiven him for the part he had played in Brenwyn's death. If not for Geoor, Edgar would have died before he could be born.

"Do you wish to leave the manor, milady?" he asked.

Morcar snapped, "Lady Cyndra will stay with me."

"I have asked *Cyndra Edgarsdottir* if she wishes to leave. Cyndra Edgarsdottir, do you wish to come with us?"

Again Sigestan's fingers bit into her shoulder. He took insult along with Morcar at hearing her name spoken in the Norse style. She wished she could tell Sigestan to remain calm. Geoor only wished to offer her a chance to escape from the hardships of living in a burgh under siege.

Cyndra hesitated. She wanted to leave; but as she looked over her shoulder at her brother, then across the hall to Cerdic and the other ceorls, she shook her head. "Geoor Scyldsson, I must tell you Cyndra Edgarsdottir cannot abandon those she cares for within these walls."

"Then I will tell my companion Edgar that she will see him when we are victorious at the end of this siege."

Cyndra clasped her hands in her lap and whispered a silent prayer. Edgar was safe. Gleineth and her husband must be, too. She had to be certain. "Edgar? Are his companions safe, also?"

"Friends of my friends are welcome always at Manor Tiwburgh." A hint of his smile was visible beneath his helmet's nosepiece. It vanished as he turned to Morcar. "If you will not change your mind, at sunrise, we attack."

"Come as you wish, you Viking dogs! You will die upon the swords of my men."

Geoor started to turn, but paused. "I will convey your message to my chieftain. He will be pleased to accept your challenge."

Morcar spat an obscenity. "You can tell Thevkil that."

"Thevkil? Chieftain Thevkil does not lead this attack. We are under the command of Chieftain Brenwyn Gunnarsson."

Cyndra gave a soft cry as she came to her feet. "He is alive?" she whispered. "Brenwyn is alive?"

"Yes."

"You told me . . . You said—"

"I told you what I knew would be true, for I have had the honor of long service with the chieftain. When he believed you were dead, milady, he thought to die in honor for his king, so he could join you in death."

"But he's alive? He truly is alive?"

Any answer Geoor might have given her was unheard as Morcar shouted for his *fyrd* to attack the emissaries. Cerdic started to repeat it; but Geoor tipped his head in a mocking salute, and with a whirl of his cape, he was gone. She knew now that Geoor had saved his startling news for last so he and his companion could escape Morcar's treachery.

As Cerdic ordered the *fyrd* to the wall, Cyndra did not move. Her brother put his hand on her arm. She looked at him and nodded when he motioned toward the back door of the hall. She hurried with him to her bur. This time, he barred the door and the window.

Cyndra did not care who heard when she cried, "Brenwyn is alive! They are under the command of Chieftain Brenwyn Gunnarsson. Canute must have promoted him. There cannot be two Brenwyn Gunnarssons." She laughed. "He is alive! And my baby is safe!"

"Cyndra, watch what you say!"

She put her fingers to her lips. She must never forget that she still was Morcar's prisoner. "I will be careful."

"Why didn't you go with Geoor Scyldsson?"

"I am the only thing that stands between the ceorls and Morcar's brutality. What do you think will happen when food becomes scarce?"

"I think if you had left, there would be one less mouth to fill."

She sank to the bench. "Sigestan, do you hate me?"

"I wish you had wed another." He sighed. "I owe Brenwyn for saving my life, but it is a debt I cannot repay when he is Chieftain Brenwyn Gunnarsson."

"He is the same man."

"Is he?" He tapped his chest. "I am who I am, and nothing will change that."

"Just as nothing will change him. He is a man of honor and loyalty who saw his family slain as you saw our father cut down. Just as you vow to avenge

Father's death, he vowed to avenge his father's. You are very much alike." She bit her lip, waiting for him to snarl back an answer at what he could see as another insult.

Slowly and with obvious reluctance, he said, "That may be so, but he is my enemy."

"He is my husband." She could not halt the smile that burst forth. "And he is alive. Do you think if I went up on the wall, I could see him?"

"Morcar will never allow that."

"I know. He will be more determined than ever to keep from losing this burgh. He might admit defeat to Geoor, but never to Brenwyn." She reached forward and grasped his hands. "He is alive, and so is Edgar. Do you think he was pleased with his son?"

"I hope he has a chance to tell you that himself before Morcar discovers a way to put an end to all of us."

The battle cries of the Jomsvikings beyond the palisades woke Cyndra. When Geoor had said they would attack at the rising of the sun, he had meant exactly that.

Pulling her robes around her, she ran out of her bur. To the east, she could see the bright arc of sunlight toying with the treetops and forcing the darkness of the night aside.

A man rushed toward her, and she turned, ready to flee back to her bur. Then she realized it was Cerdic. "Milady," he said, "you should not be out here. They are attacking."

"They will not break through the walls easily, Cerdic. Brenwyn ordered them strengthened before we left for Thevkil's stronghold."

"Now those same walls keep him out of here." He did not hide his regret.

"Do you feel you are on the wrong side?"

"One of us is, milady. Either Brenwyn or I. We have been comrades, and it is not right we should be meeting across bared swords. No, milady," he said quickly, "I will not betray my oath to protect this burgh and those within it."

She patted his arm. "Just remember that Brenwyn expects you to do as you are sworn to do."

A shout called him away. A shout from her brother. The two would work together to protect the burgh from a man they both had once called friend. She looked about, but did not see Athelbert. It was just as well. He would be useless in battle.

Cyndra went into the great hall. As she had expected, terror filled the room. She gathered together the frightened ceorls and, using the keys she wore once more, opened the chests and gave them tasks making food for the defenders and preparing for the inevitable injuries. Urging them to use work to submerge their fear, she returned to her bur to dress.

She looked at the walls. Along them, the *fyrd* was spaced evenly. The Jomsvikings must be on all sides of the manor. Brenwyn knew best how to attack Manor Darburgh, for he knew its defenses intimately. Both *fyrds* had been trained by him, and now they would do battle.

When she came into the bur, Hild was waiting. "Milady, they are here?"

"It begins, as Geoor said, at sunrise. Even Morcar cannot fail to see that the Jomsvikings can wait until we are so weak from hunger that he must surrender or die without raising a sword."

"Milady, Morcar will never surrender."

"Then he will die. And the rest of us with him."

Eighteen

Cyndra had never guessed how slowly time could pass. One week, then a fortnight, then a month passed with no change except that food grew scarce. First all the chickens were gone, then the sheep and the cows. After the horses were eaten, even the dogs vanished.

Still there was no end. A few arrows were shot from the wall; a few came over to land harmlessly in the bailey, but the siege continued.

Finally, she could no longer delay asking Cerdic the question that haunted her. "Have you seen Brenwyn?" she asked as she walked with him across the bailey.

He nodded.

"How does he look?"

"He tells me that he is well."

"You have spoken with him?"

"From the wall. Each day, he comes to the edge of their camp and calls for news of you." He lowered his voice. "Milady, it is you he wants. He cares nothing for the burgh."

She nodded with resignation. "Morcar will never give me to him. So, this will continue until we are dead. For Morcar, that will be a victory, for he will have kept Brenwyn from being with me again."

"I am afraid you are right. So, we all die, for a man we cannot admire, but to whom we are sworn."

She had no words to ease Cerdic's pain or her own as each day folded slowly into the next.

One night, screams cut through the darkness. Cyndra sat up in bed. Had the gate been battered down? Had the siege ended and the battle begun? Pulling on her tunic, she ran to her door.

Sigestan pushed her back into her bur. "Don't go out there."

"Someone is being hurt."

He scowled, his mouth working. "Someone is being killed."

"Brenwyn—"

"Not by Brenwyn. By Morcar. He decided that there were too many to feed, so he ordered the minstrels who were caught within the walls by the siege to be slain."

"He's mad!"

"You knew that, Cyndra."

She shoved past him. He grabbed for her, but she edged away. Before she had gone a half-dozen steps, her arm was grasped. She was whirled to face Morcar's contorted face.

"How can you?" she cried, then winced as another scream cut through the night.

"Would you rather starve?"

"We shall starve anyhow, if you don't put an end to this."

He twisted her arm behind her until she moaned. "You would like that, wouldn't you? Then you could scurry back to your lover's bed." He thrust her toward the ground. "Not before you warm mine."

She fought to get to her feet. Even in the dim light, she saw his hand raise. It did not fall, and she looked up to see Cerdic standing behind her.

"I must speak with you, milord," he said quietly.

"Not now."

"Now! I have a message you must see."

Morcar scowled at her as she stood, but nodded. "I will meet you in the great hall."

"It must be given to you without delay, milord."

Cyndra bit her lip, glad that Cerdic had this excuse to protect her. Or was it an excuse? What message could it be? She wanted to ask if it were from Brenwyn, but she knew better than to speak his name when Morcar was so incensed.

She gasped when Morcar seized her ring of keys and ripped them from her girdle. Stuffing them into his belt, he said, "Return to your bur, milady, and do not leave it except on my orders. Do you understand?"

"Yes."

"Yes," echoed her brother as he stepped out of the shadows. Taking her arm, he drew her back beside him. "She understands completely, and I will make sure personally that she does not disobey."

Morcar opened his mouth, then closed it, scowling. If he had thought to force her to submit when she was imprisoned in her bur alone, Sigestan's offer had deterred that plan.

Turning, she walked back to her bur. Her small victory meant nothing if Morcar continued his deadly rampage within the walls.

"Don't leave here again without me or Cerdic," Sigestan said quietly.

"We must put an end to this."

He smiled grimly, his face shadowed with an uneven growth of whiskers. Water must not be wasted, not even for shaving. "It shall end soon."

"How do you know?" She grasped his arm. "You have a plan?"

"I have been working with Cerdic—"

"He is sworn to Morcar, although he abhors him. He will not betray Morcar."

"His oath to Morcar is but one of the oaths he holds dear." He sat on the bench and looked up at her. "Two days ago, Cerdic reminded me of an oath he made to Father when you left Manor Saeburgh."

"To protect our father's blood with his life and beyond," she whispered, slowly sitting beside him. "The same vow Brenwyn took."

He nodded. "Something we hope to remind Brenwyn of when next Cerdic has a chance to speak with him across the wall. If a meeting can be arranged—"

"Without Morcar's knowledge."

"If it can be arranged, mayhap we can end this." He hesitated, then asked, "Can we trust him?"

"I believe so. Cerdic is a man of honor."

"Not Cerdic. Brenwyn."

Rising, she bit her lip. "You owe your life to Brenwyn and yet you can ask that question?"

"I must ask it." He stood and put his hands on her shoulders. "Cyndra, I must ask it. If Brenwyn's orders, as his man said, are to reclaim this manor, will he be willing to settle only for saving you? Or will he use you to obey his orders, too?"

She started to answer, sure of her answer that Brenwyn would think of her first. Then she faltered. Even though he had believed she was dead at the hand of his king, he had continued to fight for Swein and now for his son. Brenwyn loved her. She knew that, but was even her love strong enough to make him put aside his vow for vengeance?

She whispered, "I don't know."

Cyndra stood by the window of her bur and watched the setting sun's light vanish. No one was moving within the walls. Motion took energy, and energy required food. There was too little of both. Sigestan had told her how, night after night, the Jomsvikings roasted the meat they had shot in the forest. The aroma was an exquisite torture for the hungry men standing guard on the wall.

The door to the bur came crashing open. Was this part of Sigestan and Cerdic's plan or a mad scheme of Morcar's? She gripped the window's edge as she stared at Morcar. When Hild stood behind her, she was glad she was not alone to face the wrath on his face. What new way had he devised to torment her?

"Come with me, Cyndra," he ordered.

"Where?"

"You will obey, not ask questions."

She shook her head. "I will not walk calmly to my death or to watch you kill others to keep food for yourself."

"Come with me. We cannot stay here with your lover's army starving us. I think the time has come for more drastic action."

"No, I shall not scurry away with you like some sort of rodent."

He grasped her arms and pulled her roughly to the door. "I am not scurrying away. I am taking you to see your lover. How long has it been since you last saw Brenwyn Gunnarsson?"

She stared at him in astonishment. This was the

last thing she had expected. "It's been more than a year."

"A year is a very long time, milady. Do you think he still cares for you?"

"Why are you asking? He is here, isn't he?"

As he had in the forest, he struck her. Hard. She fought to keep from collapsing. "You fool," he snarled. "Why do you keep fighting when you know you are rightfully mine?"

"I am not yours. I belong first with Brenwyn." Her lips tilted, even though each motion sent renewed pain through her head. "I belong second to the abbey at Ely."

He demanded, "You continue with that lie?"

"Is it a lie, Morcar? Take me tonight, and your *fyrd* will surrender immediately in fear of heaven's fury."

He shoved her against the door. Unsteady on her feet, she crashed into it. Hild cried out and tried to rush to her lady. He halted her as Cyndra struggled to stand. She cradled her left arm in her right.

When he grasped it, she screamed, "Don't! I think it's broken."

"Soon all of you will be broken if you do not obey me." Taking her other arm, he led her across the bailey.

She did not protest, for the gate was swinging open. If Brenwyn had agreed to this, he must have some plan to rescue her and his friends within the burgh.

Torches were lit against the darkness. As Morcar pushed Cyndra ahead of him, Athelbert and his other favored thanes stood on either side to keep the Jomsvikings from trying to steal her.

The night was so silent, her breathy murmur of

Brenwyn's name seemed like a shout. She stared as he stepped forward. The year they had been parted dissolved into nothing. Several yards of empty space separated them, but all her pain vanished. Her hands longed to reach out to caress his face and the dark beard he had grown since she had last seen him. She wanted the sweetness of his mouth on her.

"We are well met, Cyndra," he said in his own language. The simple words said more than any profuse greeting.

She blinked back tears. They did not need to speak the thoughts of their hearts, which were joined together despite the miles and months apart.

She replied in the same language, although she tripped over a few words. It had been so long since she had spoken it, and her brain was slowed with the agony along her left arm. "Have you see him?" She was careful not to speak Edgar's name.

"I have, my love, and he is a fine boy. You have done so well. The king told me that you both were dead."

"Your friend beside you," she said, glancing at Geoor, "told me the same of you."

"In an effort to protect you."

"I know that now."

"And he was almost right. When I feared you were dead, I sought any duty that could lead me to death and back to your arms." He chuckled as he rested his hands on the sword that he held before him. "Instead of death, I came back, as you urged me, bathed in honor and with the blood of my enemies and a promotion to chieftain. Canute is wiser than his father, and he knows he would be a fool to put to death one of his warriors."

"I am glad."

"As I am when I stand here and see you. Our son misses his mother. When this is done, he will have a chance to learn of his father as well. And you?"

Morcar's hand tightened on her arm, so she knew she did not have much longer to speak. "I am fine. I have kept this man from my bed by telling him that I am a holy sister."

"Tell me the truth. You are hurt. Is it bad?"

"It is my arm. I think it is broken. He is not happy with my resistance. My brother will see to it." A weak smile crossed her lips. "My brother is alive."

"I have heard that, and it gladdens my heart. Will he be your ally, no matter what?"

"I don't know."

Morcar burst in, angrily. "Enough of catching up on your times apart."

Cyndra was surprised he had not interrupted before this, then realized he had been using the time to check the strength of the attackers. She doubted if he were heartened. Brenwyn's men were more numerous and better equipped than the *fyrd* within the manor.

With a snarl, Morcar said, "I see you had the gall to teach my betrothed your heathen language."

Brenwyn crossed his arms over his chest as he answered in English, "I taught my wife my language—among other pleasurable things, Morcar."

With a curse, Morcar shoved her to her knees and pressed the flat of his long knife across her throat.

"And the meaning of this brutality, Morcar?" Brenwyn asked quietly.

"I will kill her if you do not withdraw. Do you truly love her? Prove it! Leave, and take your *fyrd* with you."

"That is not my decision. King Canute has ordered me to remove you from Manor Darburgh. He did not tell me I must slay you. I gave you the opportunity once to leave alive. I offer it to you one last time."

The knife flashed, and Cyndra shrieked. A length of her hair fell to the ground.

"The next incision will be directly across her throat, chieftain. Leave here, and take your *fyrd* with you. That is an offer I make to you one last time."

Cyndra was astonished when Brenwyn hesitated, then said, "I must confer with my under-chieftains. Discussing our surrender with you is a decision we must make together."

"Please, Brenwyn," she cried, "do not give me to him. Kill me now rather than that." She moaned as Morcar wrenched her to her feet.

"Tomorrow at first light, chieftain," announced Morcar, "we will await your surrender in the great hall. I promise you that your men's deaths will not be difficult. I cannot promise the same for yours, of course." He laughed maniacally.

"Of course." Brenwyn winced as Cyndra cried out again as Morcar pulled her back into the manor. Her deepest pain was her fear for him, but he could do nothing to assuage that now.

As the gates closed and he heard the bar slip into place, Brenwyn turned. He allowed a smile to play across his lips. This had gone even better than he had expected. Tomorrow, he and his men would be allowed to enter the manor. Morcar would learn then how foolish he was to try to negotiate with the greatest traders in history.

"She has the heart of a warrior," Geoor said softly.

"A Valkyrie would be no braver. I am the one who is weak when I think of what she has suffered."

"On the morrow, she will be yours again, chieftain."

He swore plaintively. "If I only I could have been here when she returned. Cyndra has suffered too much because of me."

He remembered well his arrival at Manor Tiwburgh the day before they came to demand the surrender of Manor Darburgh. Into the hall, he had come, calling for Geoor. Stains from his long trip had darkened his garments, but he had not washed before looking for his friend.

Geoor had come across the great hall of Manor Tiwburgh with a glass of mead in each hand. "Sit and rest."

"Geoor, you call me all the way across England on this matter of utmost importance. Now you tell me to relax. Why did you send for me?"

"Calm yourself." Geoor grinned. "Ah, here is what I wanted you to see."

Brenwyn looked across the room to see a young woman carrying a child. Gleineth! What was she doing here? He had assumed, when he had not seen her at the king's court, that she had died with her lady.

Before he could greet her, Geoor took the child and held him out. "Take him, Brenwyn."

"What is this?"

"Don't you want to hold your son?"

"My son?"

"Milord," Gleineth said softly, "his name is Edgar Brenwynsson."

He took the child. The little boy, who could be no more than six or seven months old, was looking at him very seriously with eyes the same shade as his own. Gently he pushed back the golden curls on the child's head to look more closely at his face. The little boy put his thumb in his mouth and sucked it lustily.

Without raising his gaze, he asked, "What did you say his name was?" He had been so shocked to hear he had a child here at Manor Tiwburgh where he should not have one, he had not listened to the rest of Gleineth's words.

"His mother had him baptized Edgar, but she calls him Edgar Brenwynsson when she thinks no one is listening."

Brenwyn looked from the baby to Gleineth's smile. His voice broke as he gasped, "His name is *Edgar* Brenwynsson?"

Geoor laughed. "How many sons do you think you might have, my friend?"

"Cyndra?" He could say no more.

His friend eased him onto a bench. The baby stared at him as if trying to decide why this stranger was staring at him so intently. Edgar chuckled with a deep rumble in his chest as the glitter of an ornament on Brenwyn's tunic caught his attention. He grasped for it.

"Thor's hammer intrigues you, does it, my son?"

Geoor reached beneath the baby's garment and pulled out a pendant nearly identical to the one Brenwyn wore. "Mayhap he recognizes it, chieftain. He was wearing this when Gleineth and her husband brought him to Manor Tiwburgh."

The child let out a shriek of frustration at being denied his will. With a glance of apology, Gleineth took the baby and let him play with the amulet.

Brenwyn stood. "Gleineth, you have served my wife and son well. Ask what you will of me, and it will be yours."

"There is no debt." Gleineth smiled. "I am happy to serve milady."

"Where is she?" asked Brenwyn.

Gleineth grew ashen and glanced at Geoor, who shifted uneasily.

Geoor answered in a subdued voice. "With the help of Ealdorman Sigestan—"

"Cyndra's brother?"

He nodded. "He assumed his father's title. He helped Morcar regain Manor Darburgh. When Cyndra traveled with Gleineth and her husband here in hopes of finding out if her brother had come looking for her, Morcar captured Cyndra. She gave herself up to keep Morcar from learning about your son."

Brenwyn's mouth had grown as hard as the metal of his battle helmet. Cyndra had come into Morcar's possession again. Although his child was safe, Cyndra might be suffering a torment worse than one created by the ice demons of Nifelheim. It seemed the gods were determined to keep him separated from his wife.

He shook his head to clear the cloying webs of memory from his brain. In the weeks since then, he had waited for Morcar to accept the inevitable, or, more likely, for Sigestan and Cerdic to take control and throw open the gates. That had not happened. He had underestimated the hatred his apparent betrayal had caused Cyndra's brother and his friend.

Geoor tugged on his arm to break Brenwyn's gaze at the secured gate of Manor Darburgh. "The archers have returned to their positions on the wall. Someone might be eager enough to put an end to you and this siege at the same time. You can do nothing more tonight, Brenwyn."

"Don't you think I know that, Geoor? She is in there with him tonight, and I cannot help her. Her tale of becoming a nun has apparently kept him away from her, but will it work tonight as well?"

"She will do what she must."

"That is what I am fearful of."

"Come, my friend. Come. In the morning, you must be rested to rescue your wife."

This time when Geoor pulled on his arm, Brenwyn went back into their camp. The hour of the rising of the sun seemed a lifetime away as he endured the darkness alone by the fire.

Nineteen

Brenwyn smiled as he entered the great hall of Manor Darburgh. He watched for Morcar's *fyrd's* reaction to seeing him in his shining mail instead of the castoffs he had worn here and carrying his axe while his broadsword swung at his side with his steps. Murmurs of disbelief filled the room.

Perfect. He wanted them to be unsettled. That was why, when he came from the forest encampment to ask about Cyndra, he had dressed in the simple tunic all men wore. Pulling his scabbard from his belt, he raised it in a salute to them. Several started to respond, then lowered their weapons and eyes guiltily.

The ceorls were less startled. Although his uniform was now more ornate as befitted his higher rank, they had seen him as Brenwyn Gunnarsson when he captured Manor Darburgh last year. He saw relieved smiles on their faces, quickly masked, for they dared not incur Thane Morcar's wrath.

At the high table, Morcar frowned along with his men. Did they see what Brenwyn had? The *fyrd's* reaction after shock was relief much like the ceorls'.

Cyndra's face was blank, which he had expected. He fought his fury when he saw her left arm was in a sling. He cursed Morcar silently. Forcing his rage back within his heart, he knew he must not let Morcar control him even through his anger.

Looking past Cyndra, he met Sigestan's eyes. Ealdorman Sigestan. The lad had proven he was worthy of the title both at Manor Saeburgh and here, for his tales of courage had been repeated by the Jomsvikings, who had no reason to laud him. Yet, they admired this young man's determination to protect those who depended on him.

Could Cyndra depend on him today? She had been unsure, and so was Brenwyn. Sigestan must despise Morcar for what the thane had done to her, but his loyalty was to the hapless English king.

Raising his sword again, Brenwyn handed it to Geoor, who balanced it across his arms. He was determined to continue with ceremony as long as possible to keep Morcar and his favored thanes busy. Because Morcar thrived on protocol, this might be the best way to create the needed diversion.

"Greetings, Morcar, thane of Manor Darburgh," he said.

Morcar scowled, clearly hating to have to reply with the same courtesy. "Greetings to you, Brenwyn Gunnarsson, chieftain of Canute."

Brenwyn's eyebrows arched at the lack of title given to his king, but he said, "Greetings to you also, Ealdorman Sigestan."

"And to you, Chieftain Brenwyn Gunnarsson." His voice was cold. Because of his fury at Morcar or his hatred for the Jomsvikings? Brenwyn wished he knew.

"Greetings to you, Cyndra Edgarsdottir." By using that name, he announced that he would not relinquish her as his wife.

"Welcome to Manor Darburgh, Brenwyn." She did not give him a title, the omission making her words as intimate as a caress.

"The pleasantries are over, chieftain," Morcar snarled. "Are you ready to surrender, or do you wish to see Cyndra slain before your eyes?"

Sigestan snarled, "You shall not kill her!"

At his quick order, Athelbert drew his sword and held it against Sigestan's chest. Cyndra took a step to halt him, but Morcar seized her arm. She moaned in pain.

"I have said I would be willing to discuss surrender." The pleasant Brenwyn disappeared to be replaced by the fierce Jomsviking. "I said nothing of surrendering my men to you."

Cyndra was the only one on the high platform not astounded by the metamorphosis. She had seen it often. Both men were Brenwyn. She glanced at Morcar. His eyes revealed that panic was rising to bewash his mind. Clearly he had not, even in the darkest depths of his depraved mind, envisioned his ceorl as the powerful warrior who had been made a chieftain by his king.

"Slay him now," he growled.

She looked at Brenwyn, then realized he was looking behind her. She whirled and grasped Athelbert's arm as it rose to drive his sword into her brother.

"Don't kill him!" she cried.

Throughout the room, shouts echoed hers.

Brenwyn pulled his sword from its sheath and leaped forward to place the point of his blade in the center of Athelbert's nape. "Rescind your order, Morcar, or this thane will die before the ealdorman does."

The thane chuckled. "You care so for a man who would see you dead for betraying his father?"

"Brenwyn did not betray our father." Cyndra was glad Athelbert was too much of a coward to challenge Brenwyn. "He saved Sigestan and me once, and any information he had about Manor Saeburgh he never sent to his commander."

"Is this true?" Sigestan asked, his eyes narrowing.

"Yes, it is true," Brenwyn answered quietly. "I swear it by my sword-sworn oath, just as I swear before everyone here that nothing is more important to me than your sister."

Cyndra whispered, "Not even your vengeance?"

"What value is vengeance if it steals the very thing I have sought?" He tipped his sword so it caught the light, but still held it to the thane's neck as he said, "I swear before all these witnesses that nothing matters more to me than the love that you have brought to me, Cyndra."

Morcar sneered, "Such an oath has little value."

"You shall see how much value it has if you do not order your thane to lower his sword, for I swear I shall run him through."

Morcar shouted, "Cerdic, kill that Viking bastard!"

Cerdic opened his mouth, then closed it.

"I told you! Order them to kill that Viking!"

The *fyrd* looked to Cerdic to relay Morcar's order. The ceorl kept his eyes securely on Sigestan's face. Cyndra held her breath. As Morcar shrieked his orders a third time, she continued to stare at Cerdic. Could it be that he would not raise his sword against Brenwyn? No, it was not for that reason, although the two men had been friends. She knew he would not break his oath to her father to protect his blood.

If he were to kill Brenwyn, then Athelbert would slay Sigestan.

Brenwyn called, "To whom are you sworn, Cerdic?"

Cerdic's gaze did not flicker, but his head rose as he walked to the wall and pulled off his shield. Taking it, he threw it to the floor. He raised his foot and drove it down into the shield, cracking it.

Morcar swore at the ceorl's public breaking of his oath of allegiance to Manor Darburgh. "Cerdic, you—"

"My only oath," Cerdic said, coming back to stand by the others in the *fyrd,* "is to protect our lady and her blood, chieftain."

"And who has your heart and fealty, Cyndra?"

"All that is mine is yours." She smiled when she spoke the words of a sword-sworn oath.

Brenwyn continued to look at Morcar and hold his sword against Athelbert as he said, "I say to the men of the *fyrd* of Manor Darburgh who are loyal to their lady and her blood, rid yourselves of your weapons. Those who accept the rightful rule of King Canute Sweinsson will be unharmed."

A sound like hail filled the hall as the *fyrd* dropped their weapons to the floor.

Athelbert lunged away from Brenwyn's sword. With the table between them, Brenwyn could not halt him. Sigestan leaped aside, pushing Cyndra behind him as he drew his blade. As Brenwyn jumped on the platform and onto the table, Sigestan sliced into Athelbert. The thane fell back, striking the table and knocking Brenwyn to the floor.

Cyndra ran toward the back door. A claw grasped her arm. Morcar!

"Let me go!" she cried.

"No, milady. You will never return to your lover while I live!" He whirled her against him, raising his knife once more to her throat. "Brenwyn! It's time to put an end to this."

Brenwyn climbed up onto the platform, stepping over Athelbert's body. He put his hand on Sigestan's shoulder. The young man hesitated, then gripped his arm as an ally. Noting how Morcar's eyes narrowed at the motion, Brenwyn walked closer.

"Stay back," Morcar ordered.

Leaning on his sword that bit deeply into the floor, he gazed at the thane. He was as composed as if they were about to discuss the day's activities, as they had so often when Brenwyn had pretended to be his ceorl.

The thane readily ordered, "Tell your Jomsvikings to lay down their weapons. Do it now if you want Cyndra to live. Delay, and she will die!"

"Give me Cyndra Edgarsdottir, and we shall leave."

"Do you think me a fool?" he snorted. "I give my betrothed to you, and you will raze Manor Darburgh."

"You have my word. Manor Darburgh will stand, but only if you give me Cyndra and her allies."

Morcar spat at the floor. "That is what I think of your word, Chieftain Brenwyn Gunnarsson. You and all your Jomsvikings will rot in hell before I give her to you."

Brenwyn was amazed when Cyndra asked, "Morcar, didn't you tell me when you brought me here that you wished Brenwyn were alive? You told me you regretted not having the chance to kill him yourself."

Brenwyn laughed in derision. "You must have misunderstood him, Cyndra, my love. Even Morcar would not be stupid enough to suggest he could best me in one-on-one combat."

"I am saying only what he said."

"I still say you must be in error," continued Brenwyn, watching the knife at her throat. He had to make sure he did not push the thane too far. Then Morcar might kill Cyndra out of spite. "This thane would not dare to brag of beating a Jomsviking when he knows he could not."

Morcar snarled, "Clear the hall of your Vikings and this pitiful *fyrd* you trained to be cowards. Then we shall see who is the victor."

Cyndra gasped. She had expected Morcar to accept defeat, not this challenge. She saw her disbelief mirrored on Brenwyn's face.

"Scared, Brenwyn Gunnarsson?" taunted the thane. "Is that why you hesitate? Do you want to lengthen the short time you have left on this earth? Do as I say, or I will rid us both of this lady now."

Brenwyn swept his hand out in a wide motion and snapped an order in both English and the Norse language. When Geoor hesitated, Brenwyn shouted something Cyndra did not understand. Slowly the hall emptied. Beyond the walls, they could hear the sounds of the Jomsvikings ordering the ceorls and *fyrd* from the hall. Inside there was only silence.

"As you requested, Morcar," Brenwyn said quietly. "Now we can fight, if you wish to be that stupid, or you can simply surrender to me."

"Surrender to you? Never! You shall be the one dead soon."

His eyes bulging with fury, Morcar shoved Cyndra aside. He ignored her gasp as she hit a wall. Brenwyn wanted to ask if she were all right, but Morcar already was moving toward him.

Morcar's blade slashed in a deadly arc. Brenwyn easily eluded it.

Only Brenwyn's desire to let Cyndra emerge alive kept the battle from being over immediately. He wanted to give her time to flee. In the center of the room around the fire pit, he parried every motion Morcar made, but did not press any opportunity to attack.

Again and again, he said, "Morcar, surrender now!"

Morcar panted, but snarled, "Never!"

Brenwyn could tell the thane was tiring, for his swings were becoming more erratic. His eyes swept the room as he deflected every blow. Geoor must have followed his order to get Cyndra out of here as soon as this battle began. He heard some commotion outside, but knew his men could handle it. He needed to put an end to this.

When he backed Morcar into a corner, the thane proved more agile than he had guessed. Morcar pushed a cask of mead toward him. Brenwyn leaped out of the way. He heard the barrel crash behind him. Seeing the triumph in Morcar's mad eyes, he risked a glance over his shoulder.

The cask had broken by the fire pit, and the mead was flowing toward the fire. If it did not drown the flames, it would ignite the hall.

"Surrender, Morcar!" he demanded. "Let us be done with this before we are burned alive."

"Afraid of a bit of fire?"

Brenwyn clenched his teeth. Did Morcar know his weakness, his nightmares of seeing his family burned alive? Praise Odin that Cyndra was out of here!

Morcar swung his sword once again. "You will die, even if I have to die with you."

As the swords clanged together, Brenwyn jumped away from the blazing tongue licking at the wine spilled across the floor. He backed away from the fire that was flirting with the walls. Morcar followed to press his attack.

Brenwyn kept his eyes on his enemy's face. His brow furrowed when he saw another flash of victory in Morcar's eyes. His foot slipped on a forgotten sword. As he dropped to the floor, he heard Morcar's exultant shout. He raised his sword to plunge it into Brenwyn.

"Die, Viking dog!"

Brenwyn drove his sword up at the very moment of Morcar's cry of victory. The thane stared at him in amazement, then fell to the floor as Brenwyn rolled away.

Something pricked Brenwyn's hand. He jumped to his feet and whirled to face this new attacker. Then he realized it had been a spark from the fire that was halfway to the thatched roof. Once reaching it, the flames would explode and rain down fire to kill anyone within the hall.

Choking from the smoke that clogged his throat, he reeled out of the hall. Let Morcar have his funeral pyre. Two men rushed forward to help him, but he waved them aside. Several breaths of the fresh air would revive him.

"Morcar is dead?" Geoor asked.

Brenwyn nodded and pointed with his bloody sword toward the hall. "The fool was determined to die."

"And Cyndra?"

"Cyndra!" His head snapped up. "You were to

bring her out as soon as Morcar took his first swing at me."

"There was trouble. I—I—"

"Enough!" He looked at the people staring at the fire. He did not see her golden hair. "She is still in there!"

Geoor put out his hand. "You can't! It's too late, Brenwyn!"

"I lost my family to the madness of English flames. No one else I love is going to be burned alive!" He ran back into the hall. "Cyndra!"

Beneath the table on the raised platform, Cyndra heard her name being shouted. She tried to breathe. She could not. She started to rise, but cried out in agony as she put weight on her broken arm.

She heard a crackle. Fire! She had to get out of here. She tried again to stand, then realized the smoke was not as thick near the floor. Pulling her veil over her mouth, she retched. She had to get out of here.

Fighting her panic, she struggled to figure out where she was on the platform. The door was either a dozen paces to the right or the left. If she made the wrong decision, she could wander in the smoke until she died.

A hand grasped hers and drew her toward a form only slightly visible in the smoke. "Cyndra?"

"Sigestan!" she rasped. "We must get out of here. The back door is this way."

"No, Cyndra. There is a wall of flame between here and there. We must go out the front door." He tugged on her hand. Pain swept up her other arm, but she ignored it.

She gripped the back of his tunic and lurched after him. She heard her name shouted again.

"Dear God!" she moaned. "That's Brenwyn! Is he in here, too?"

"Don't stop," Sigestan ordered.

She opened her mouth to shout to Brenwyn, but the crack of wood eclipsed every other sound. The roof timbers must be breaking. They had to get out of here! Brenwyn! Where was Brenwyn? Only when Sigestan shoved Cyndra away from him, did she realize the roof was caving in.

"No!" she screamed as, in a flash of fire, she saw her brother fall beneath the flaming beams. "Sigestan!"

She screamed again as the fire leaped up from the floor to surround her. Sinking to her knees, she fought to breathe, but could not. Tears of grief and pain flowed down her cheeks as all thoughts vanished from her brain. She dropped senseless on the floor. Her last whispered breath was Brenwyn's name.

Epilogue

The burgh was ready for the festival that would begin with the dawn. By tomorrow evening, the lanterns that had been hung from the trees would challenge the glow of the stars. There would be music and voices gathered around the fire pit, where a pig roasted and freshly cooked venison and mutton waited to be put on overfilled plates.

But now it was quiet.

Brenwyn stood at the window of the bedchamber in the stone hall that had been raised through the past three years. It was built atop the ashes of Morcar's hall and would not fall easily. He glanced toward the outer wall, where the watch walked off the hours, still cautious although, for the first time in generations, peace claimed the English countryside. On the morrow, Manor Darburgh would celebrate the tidings of the marriage of Canute Sweinsson to Emma, the widow of the late King Ethelred.

When he had offered to return to England five years ago to do Swein Forkbeard's bidding to claim all of this island for his king, Brenwyn had not thought he would live to see a day when this peace would reign. He had been even less sure of that on the day when he had feared all he loved was once more doomed to the flame.

He wondered if he would ever be able to forget the nightmare of going back into Morcar's burning hall to seek Cyndra, knowing how small the chances were of getting to her in time. It had been like entering the nether regions of fiery hell. With his tunic over his mouth to protect himself from the thick ravages of the smoke, he had pushed through the smoke. Only his desire to find Cyndra had kept him from fleeing the inferno.

A voice from the inner bailey rose to his window, and he smiled. Sigestan! In the wake of Morcar's death, Sigestan had remained here, knowing there was nothing for him to return to on the lands that once had belonged to Manor Saeburgh. His acceptance of Brenwyn as rightful lord of Manor Darburgh had allowed Cerdic and the *fyrd* to swear their allegiance to him as well. Since that day, the lad had proven he was as able an administrator as his father.

Brenwyn rested his chin on his palm while he balanced his elbow on the wide sill. Fortunately, for Cyndra's brother, Brenwyn had stumbled upon Sigestan as he sought Cyndra. He had not known her brother had gone into the building, although he should have guessed not even the risk of such a terrible death would break the bonds of love between Ealdorman Edgar's children. When he found Sigestan, a beam with fire racing along it pinned the lad to the floor. It had not crushed him, for the long table had taken the force of its fall.

The call of the hour from the watch faded into silence as Brenwyn remembered how he had rushed to the door to shout for help to save Sigestan. His Jomsvikings and the manor's ceorls together had braved the fire to assist him. Then he had turned to face the wall of flames that taunted him to recall how he had come back to his village too late to save his family.

"Why are you standing here by the window? You will need every bit of your energy tomorrow to dance from dawn until the following dawn." Slender arms swept up across his chest as soft hair brushed his back.

Smiling, he closed the shutters on the window and turned so those arms curved around his back. The moonlight found its way around the shutters to spin gold through that long hair as he bent to taste the lips that were all the sweeter because, even three years later, he could not forget how close he had come to losing this woman . . . again.

Cyndra laughed and stepped away. He tugged her back to him, burying his face in her hair.

"Is something wrong?" she whispered, her fingers brushing his face tenderly.

"Not now, my sweet lady." He savored the scent of her skin's own soft perfume to banish the smothering smoke that still clung to his memories. If he had not chanced upon Sigestan in the burning hall, the lad never would have been able to lead him to where Cyndra was senseless in the smoke. He knew, in that inferno, alone he would never have found her in time.

She had suffered from the smoke for several weeks, but had recovered to welcome her husband and their son back into her life. Her first smile as she woke in his arms had cast out all the darkness that had claimed his heart for so many years. He had had his revenge, although it had nearly demanded of him the greatest treasure any man could possess. He wanted nothing but to live with his wife and their children and their children's children in peace and love.

His hand caressed her gently rounded abdomen where their second child was growing strong. When her fingers covered his, he raised his head to look down into her luminous eyes. He never would tire of gazing at her. The horror that had separated them for so long and so nearly forever was gone, but made each moment they shared all the more precious.

"The baby sleeps, Brenwyn," she whispered. "You should as well."

"I have no thoughts of sleeping now."

"You have worried too much about the celebration tomorrow. There will be no trouble. Everyone within these walls and beyond has sworn allegiance to you and to the new king. It is time to forget the past and celebrate the future." She took his hand and stepped toward the wide bed that was a grand as the one they had shared in Thevkil's stronghold. The closed door beyond it led to their son's room. "You must stop fretting about all the plans for the celebration."

"That is not what is keeping me awake." With a low chuckle, he gathered her up into his arms. He kissed her with deep, unhurried longing as she wrapped her arms around his shoulders. As he crossed the room, carrying her against his chest, he said, "You should be in bed."

"You worry too much about me, too. I bore Edgar in that primitive hut along the eastern sea with only Gleineth's help, so you need not cosset me with this second child. Gleineth is here to help me again."

"Now, you shall do nothing to risk yourself. While

this is your second child, you must remember it is the first chance I have had to agonize about all the little things that happen with a baby."

"It will be easier for both of us with the next."

He smiled as he leaned her back on the soft bed. Kneeling over her, he whispered, "I like how you think, milady."

"And I like how you love me, milord." As he reached for the laces on her undertunic, she whispered, "I never could have imagined my life would take this path, but I am so glad it has."

"So that you would become the wife of one of your hated enemies?"

"You were never my enemy." She smiled as she ran her hands along his thighs. When his breath caught in the need that was sated only in her sweet touch, she murmured, "Well, mayhap you were my enemy at one time, but you were always my beloved enemy."

"I vow that you will always be simply my beloved, Cyndra." He slowly drew apart the laces on her tunic.

"And you never make a vow you might break?"

"Never." He smiled in the moment before his lips covered hers, sealing this vow in the sweetest way they knew.